W
Bo   Boggs, Johnny D.
      Hannah and the Horseman

No._____

THREE OAKS TOWNSHIP LIBRARY

Three Oaks, Michigan

RULES

1. Books may be kept for two weeks and can be renewed; 7-day books and magazines are so designated.

2. A fine of five cents a day will be charged on books which are not returned according to the above rule. No book will be issued to any person incurring such a fine until it has been paid.

3. All injuries to books beyond reasonable wear and all losses shall be made good to the satisfaction of the Librarian.

4. Each borrower is held responsible for all books drawn on his card and for all fines accrucruing on the same.

HANNAH
AND THE
HORSEMAN

HANNAH
AND THE
HORSEMAN

•

JOHNNY D. BOGGS

AVALON BOOKS
THOMAS BOUREGY AND COMPANY, INC.
401 LAFAYETTE STREET
NEW YORK, NEW YORK 10003

© Copyright 1997 by Johnny D. Boggs
Library of Congress Catalog Card Number: 96-95479
ISBN 0-8034-9230-8

PRINTED IN THE UNITED STATES OF AMERICA
ON ACID-FREE PAPER
BY HADDON CRAFTSMEN, SCRANTON, PENNSYLVANIA

For my parents,
Darrell C. Boggs and Jackie McGee Boggs

Chapter One

He slammed into the hard juniper fence, almost cracking his ribs, flipped over the top rail, and crashed onto the rocky ground with a thud. What little breath he had whooshed from his lungs, and he lay there on his back, spread-eagled, eyes closed, wondering how the day had suddenly turned out so wrong.

One horse. That's all he had left to break, and he could leave his rawhide camp for town, enjoy a cigar and a beer and a feather bed. But that one horse was a strong, black stallion sixteen hands high—tall for a mustang—with a streak of vengeance like a Greek god. "A widow-maker." That's what the old bronc-busters would call him.

Pete Belissari was a first-generation American. His father, who had been a poor Greek fisherman in Piraeus, now was a ship's captain in Corpus

1

Christi, Texas, where his mother taught school and his sister was married to a doctor. Pete was twenty-eight years old, had a college education, and could speak Greek, English, Spanish and even some Apache. Yet here he was, in the rugged mountains of West Texas, trying to break wild mustangs and sell them to the United States Army at seventy-five dollars a head.

He groaned and slowly sat up, testing his ribs first and then gently probing the knot on his forehead. He woke up this morning feeling refreshed, enjoyed a leisurely breakfast of coffee and hardtack and a few pages of Homer, then got to work, roping and saddling the black mustang and jumping into the saddle only to be thrown time and time again. It was hard work, but seventy-five bucks was more than most men made in two months, and Belissari had been in the mountains for only two months. With nine mustang mares already broken, Belissari had six hundred and seventy-five dollars waiting to be spent—providing he could get the horses to Fort Davis.

He could give up on the stallion, but surrender wasn't in Belissari's vocabulary. Besides, he had lasted two minutes on the black this last ride. Maybe he was wearing down that "widow-maker."

The mustang snorted, Belissari picked up his hat, glared at the horse, and limped away from the make-shift corral to his bedroll and possibles. He took a long pull from his canteen, the water spilling and wetting his coarse beard. He slapped the dust off his hat against his legs and settled it back on his dark head. And then he saw the flash.

Sunlight had reflected off something in the rocks above. A rifle? At least it was something man-made.

That could mean trouble. He studied the rough, mountainous terrain carefully, searching for another flash or movement. With all the nooks and crannies in the rocks, juniper and piñon, a man could easily hide up there. This was Apache country, and although there hadn't been much Indian trouble in two years, it paid to be careful. Besides, there was also the possibility of bandits, and Roland Kibbee, a trader in the Davis Mountains, was known to steal a horse now and then.

An owl hooted in the distance.

And that, Belissari knew, meant real trouble. An owl at two in the afternoon?

He had just drunk a pint of water, but now his mouth was parched. Pete Belissari studied his camp. His Winchester .44–40 carbine was leaning against the corral; his Colt .45 was in the belted holster by his bedroll. Wearing a gun belt while breaking horses was awkward at best, stupid at worst, and Pete Belissari was neither awkward nor stupid. Slowly, calmly, he bent over and drew the short-barreled revolver from the leather holster. He pulled the hammer to half cock, opened the chamber gate, and rotated the cylinder, the metallic clicks drowned out by the pounding of Belissari's heart. He checked the five loads— for only a fool carried six bullets in a revolver—and shoved the Colt into the holster, buckling the gun belt around his waist as he stood up.

He moved quickly, but not in a panic, as he gathered his essential belongings—his book of Homer, canteen, bedroll, and war bag—and strapped them behind his saddle, which he then threw on his gray horse, Poseidon. The owl sounded again, and Belissari quickened his pace, leaping into the corral as the black mustang reared and roared. He deftly roped the animal and tied it up short against a fence post. This was stupid, he thought, but he couldn't leave the animal like this. Besides, if the Apaches wanted this mustang, they'd have to work as hard as he did for it. He removed the saddle and bridle and kicked open the gate, then unfastened the lariat and screamed his best Johnny Reb war cry and the mustang galloped out of the corral and out of his camp.

"Some other time," Belissari said as he picked up the lariat and darted out of the corral himself, grabbing his Winchester but leaving the saddle and bridle behind. He went into the other corral he had built to hold his saddle-ready mustangs and slipped loops over their necks to pull them behind his horse.

He was walking briskly toward Poseidon when he saw the Apache.

He stood on top of the ridge above, in full view, sunlight bouncing off the metal blade of his long lance. He wore a fringed deerskin shirt, leggings and moccasins, and had a blue-and-white checked table-cloth wrapped around his waist. On his head was a dark, open-topped fur turban, decorated with feathers and beads. He stood unafraid, staring at Belissari below.

Mescalero, Belissari thought as he rested the rifle barrel against his shoulder. It wasn't a threatening move, but Belissari wanted this Apache to know that he wasn't afraid. Of course, Pete Belissari was afraid—only a fool or a dead man wouldn't be. The two men studied each other for long seconds. Belissari blinked and the Apache disappeared.

He let out a deep breath and hurried to Poseidon,

shoving the Winchester into the scabbard and swinging into the saddle. He loped to the corral, opened the
gate, and grabbed the end of the lariat, pulling his
nine horses behind him and leaving the Apaches some
horse tack, coffee, pots, pans, and anything else he
didn't have time to pack.

It was hard going down the narrow mountain trails.
Belissari leaned back in the saddle, holding the string
of horses in his left hand and butt of his revolver in
his right. His reins were held by his teeth, but Poseidon was twelve years old and didn't need much guidance. He probably was scared of the Mescalero
Apaches too.

At the bottom of the trail, to get to the open ground,
he had to pass through a narrow canyon. He reined
to a stop and let the horses catch their breath, then
kicked Poseidon's sides with his soft deerskin moccasins. They were undecorated and calf high—
Apache style.

As a horseman, Pete Belissari didn't believe in using spurs and quirts. That made him a rarity among
Texas horse drovers, most of whom would rake the
spirit out of a horse with sharp rowels. The less violent method worked for Belissari, though. He had
caught Poseidon in the mountains five years ago, broken him, and kept him rather than sell him to the
Army. And Poseidon had never let him down.

"Easy, boy," Belissari said as the horse walked
forward. The high walls blocked the sun's warmth
and cast a cold, deathlike shadow across the
horseman's body. He pulled the Colt from its holster
and thumbed back the hammer, the horses' hooves
clopping on the hard rock and echoing through the

canyon. The path was less than twenty-five yards, but it felt like miles to Belissari. One Apache above could pick him off easily. *Is this worth six hundred and seventy-five dollars?* Belissari thought, holding his breath.

Poseidon reached the end of the canyon and took his rider and train of horses into the bright, vast country of West Texas. The sun warmed Belissari's face and his spirits; he holstered his revolver and exhaled deeply.

The country before him was broken and desolate, strewn with boulders, gullies, and pockets of brush and yucca. In the distance, other mountains rose into the cloudless, blue sky. Belissari knew he was far from safety, but it sure felt good to be out of the mountains, where a man would be hard-pressed to run. The country before him was like the sea, and he felt like Homer's Odysseus, about to sail off to adventure.

A gunshot snapped him back to reality.

The bullet zipped past his neck, tugging at his red bandanna and causing Poseidon to buck twice. Belissari barely could keep hold of the rope, and the mustangs screamed and danced while Belissari tried to stay in the saddle. Poseidon quickly calmed, however, and Belissari took the reins from his teeth, but even before he could kick his horse or scream, Poseidon understood and was loping away as the second bullet spanged off a boulder.

His hat flew off his head but was saved by the rawhide stampede string, which tugged at Belissari's throat as the Stetson danced on his back. The lariat pulling the horses burned Belissari's left hand and the horses' weight seemed to be pulling his arm out of his shoulder socket.

Belissari glanced back to see a band of Apaches pouring out of the mountains. He saw a white puff of smoke and heard the report of a rifle but felt no bullet. Kicking Poseidon harder, he turned around. The big gray was a solid horse and excellent swimmer, but Belissari knew he probably couldn't outrun the Apache—especially not with him pulling along nine other horses.

He studied the countryside, but West Texas didn't offer much encouragement, even in 1884. The nearest settlement was Fort Davis—a hard two-day ride away—and he didn't have much hope of running into a scouting patrol. Another rifle shot sounded. Closer. They were gaining on him. He turned back quickly to get a count. Nine. No, ten.

Ahead of him stood a dark outcropping of reddish gray volcanic rocks overlooking an arroyo. Belissari pulled on the reins, Poseidon slowed, and he eased the horse down into the arroyo, pulling the horses behind him. He swung from the saddle, wrapped the lariat around the saddle horn, and pulled the Winchester from the scabbard, then scrambled up the rocks, jacking a shell into the carbine's chamber and kneeling against the boulder.

The Apaches were galloping toward him, but if he could show them that he meant to fight, maybe they would stop. So far, they hadn't proved to be much good at shooting. He took aim and fired, and the Indians turned, racing off, trying to flank him, he guessed, rather than charge him straight on.

They were about two hundred yards away, so Belissari adjusted the rear sight of his Winchester and levered a fresh cartridge into the carbine. He glanced at the horses below, pleased to see they hadn't moved. To be afoot in this country meant death.

"Good job, Poseidon," he said softly and looked back toward the Apaches.

A Mescalero had stopped his horse and dismounted. He was standing behind the horse, resting a rifle on the horse's back. Smoke belched and the bullet screamed less than an inch from Belissari's head, banged into the boulder, and splintered. A chuck of rock cut Belissari's bearded face and sent him flying facedown into the dirt.

The Mescalero's second shot kicked dirt into his eyes and blinded him. Belissari was backing away, shaking his head and blinking rapidly, trying to regain his vision. The third shot cut across his ribs, tearing his navy flannel shirt and sending him tumbling into the arroyo.

He had to move fast. He couldn't outshoot this Mescalero, and the others would have him flanked—trapped—if he didn't hurry.

"Come on!" he said, hugging the ground, fighting the blackness until his vision returned, blurred and painful, but he could see enough to run. He shoved the Winchester into the scabbard and pulled himself into the saddle, leaning forward to make him less of a target, and kicked the horse into a run.

He climbed out of the arroyo on the far side and could hear the Mescaleros coming closer. Belissari bit his lower lip and dropped the lariat, letting his nine mustangs—his six hundred and seventy-five dollars of backbreaking work—go. Poseidon picked up speed, and he heard the Apaches shout. His vision was much better now, so he looked back.

The Indians weren't pursuing him. They had captured his string of horses and were shouting and celebrating, shooting rifles into the air. He let Poseidon keep at a gallop, though, and felt his ribs, where the bullet had torn his shirt. He wasn't hurt, but on he ran until he was out of the Apaches' sight.

He dismounted and drank heartily from his canteen, then filled his hat and let Poseidon drink. "Rest," he told Poseidon as he pulled off the saddle and stretched out in the rocks. "We've got a lot of work to do tonight."

Chapter Two

Belissari thought about taking a nap, knowing he would be busy that night, but the proximity of the Apaches ruled out sleep. First, he cleaned his rifle. Next, he found *The Odyssey* and read for about an hour. Once, Belissari had also owned a copy of Homer's *The Iliad,* but he had left it on a rock and Poseidon dined on about three hundred pages while he was breaking a mustang.

Finally, Pete Belissari rose and scouted the area until he found what he needed, a patch of purplish plants growing near the rocks. He cropped the weeds, wrapping them in paper, and with a smile shoved them into his war bag. Locoweed.

If ten Mescalero Apaches think they can get away with stealing my mustangs, Belissari said to himself, *they have made a serious blunder.* In a few minutes,

10

Belissari and Poseidon were riding back toward the arroyo, where he easily picked up the trail of the Indians.

He thought of sitting in Captain Vernon Kaye's office at Fort Davis after his friend, and biggest customer, had examined the stock of mustangs.

"Whose brand are they wearing?" Kaye would ask.

Belissari would smile and reply, "Well, mostly I'm wearing theirs." And he would point to his latest scar, cut, or bruise.

Kaye would add, "I'd say that by tomorrow they'll be wearing a U.S. brand. How 'bout a shot of ouzo to celebrate?"

And Vernon Kaye would hand over a voucher for payment and a shot of forty-rod whiskey—not the clear Greek beverage ouzo. But Pete Belissari would choke it down, smiling.

The sealing of the deal had become a running gag between the two friends. And if the horseman recaptured his mustangs from the Apaches, he would have a fine story to tell Kaye.

So Pete Belissari followed the Apache trail back to the mountains. The Apaches weren't even making an effort to hide their tracks, which meant they figured no one man would pursue ten Mescaleros. Poseidon's iron shoes rang against the hard stone of the rugged range, so Belissari dismounted and found four thick rabbit pelts in his war bag. He wrapped these around the hooves, fastening them with leather thongs, then climbed back into the saddle and kicked Poseidon forward.

Dusk came quickly in the high country but

Belissari wasn't worried. Even though the tracks had disappeared on the granite rocks, a herd of fleeing mustangs and ten unshod Indian ponies was easy to follow. Clipped branches. Scarred rock. A loose stone. Torn pieces of calico and muslin. Even a dab of blood. Belissari knew what to look for. Dusk faded to the blackness of night, but the moon rose quickly and gave him enough light to follow the trail.

He smelled the campfire long before he heard the laughter of the Indians. Glancing at the stars, he guessed that it was about ten o'clock. He swung from the saddle, pulling the Winchester from the scabbard, and hobbled Poseidon's forefeet. The gray stallion probably wouldn't wander off, but the horseman couldn't take any chances.

"I'll be back, boy," he said softly, disappearing into the brush, climbing silently up a deer trail until he dropped underneath a stunted juniper and looked at the camp below.

The Apaches were gathered around a campfire, laughing and drinking whiskey and coffee; the aroma of the coffee caused Belissari's stomach to knot. On a flat rise above them, on a clearing about thirty yards from the camp, the mustangs and the Indian ponies were held in a rope corral. Belissari saw the off-and-on glow of a cigarette near the corral. One guard there. He counted eight Apaches by the fire. That left one more sentry. But where?

A twig snapped behind him, and Belissari froze. His hands felt clammy against the cold Winchester he held, and he began to sweat profusely. Then he saw the Indian, standing right beside him, a battered Springfield rifle cradled in his arms. He was barely a boy, maybe fourteen, wearing moccasins, deerskin britches, muslin shirt, and gingham headband. The kid was looking at the campfire longingly, so close that Belissari could almost touch him without moving.

He knew he couldn't shoot—a gunshot would send the rest of the camp into a frenzy. Nor could he move to find his knife—any movement would alert the boy to his presence. Besides, the last thing Pete Belissari wanted to do was kill someone. All he wanted was his horses.

This was a game to the Indians, Belissari knew. Steal some horses from the enemies and celebrate. They had probably left the reservation in New Mexico to have some fun. And stealing horses from a white man was a lot of fun.

Pete Belissari moved quickly. He stepped forward in a flash, and the Mescalero boy, eyes wide, backed up and opened his mouth to scream. The stock of the Winchester carbine crashed against the Apache's temple and he dropped like a rock, the rifle clanging on the rocks, a noise that seemed deafening to the mustang hunter.

He sucked in air and held his breath as he knelt by the unconscious Indian. His heart pounded, but laughter still sounded from the Apache camp. He peered below cautiously, then let out a silent breath. They hadn't heard the rifle hit the rocks. Quickly Belissari wiped his sweaty brow, dried his hands on his trousers, and gagged the Indian boy with his headband. He cut away a shirtsleeve and tied the kid's hands behind his back, tossed the Springfield into the bushes, and moved back down to Poseidon.

He led his horse around the hills and through the

trees until he was maybe fifty yards from the rope corral, scouting out a path of retreat in the darkness. Again, he hobbled the stallion and moved forward in a crouch to find the second sentry. He saw the Mescalero rolling another cigarette beside the rope corral. This is easy, Belissari thought.

Then Poseidon whinnied. And the Apache whirled and cocked his Winchester. Belissari disappeared behind a rock and bit his bottom lip. One of the mustang mares in the corral snorted and whinnied in return. He could feel the approaching Indian, but couldn't hear his moccasins. Sweat returned. He felt his heart pounding against his chest. And then the rifle barrel of the Apache appeared inches from his face . . . pointed, however, in the direction of Poseidon. Quickly Belissari dropped his Winchester and grabbed the enemy's barrel, pulling it forward and sticking out his right foot. The Mescalero yelped in surprise as he was jerked forward. He tripped and fell sprawling to the ground, losing his rifle. Belissari was on top of him in an instant, both hands clamped around the Indian's throat, preventing another scream. The Indian was also a young boy. He thrashed violently but couldn't free himself and finally passed out.

Belissari released his grip and again bound and gagged the sentry. He cast a menacing glare in Poseidon's direction, then dashed toward the horse. "Thanks, pal," he whispered sarcastically as he unfastened the hobble and led his mount to the rope corral. His horses were still tied together with his lariat. He looked at the Apache ponies and for a second considered adding them to his herd. But he decided that ten extra horses would slow him down.

So he found the locoweed, eased into the makeshift corral and gave each Apache pony several bites, careful not to give them lethal dosages. By the time he left, the animals would be bloating, rolling on the ground, snorting, unable to be ridden, and generally acting loco. It would be hours before they could pursue him. And at this, Belissari smiled with pleasure. He was pulling his animals out of the corral, when he heard the shout.

He looked forward and saw an Apache drop a cup of coffee and point a bony finger in his direction. Of all the luck, Belissari thought, and stepped forward, jacking a shell into his carbine.

"Help me, Apollo," he said drily.

The Winchester barked and the Apache dived for cover. The mustangs jumped, but Belissari ignored them and ran a few yards forward. He fired another shot at the nearest Indian and put two slugs into the campfire to scatter the others.

And then he saw one Apache stand up, bringing a heavy rifle to his shoulder. It was an old Henry rifle with a long, brass telescopic sight fastened to the barrel. It had to be the same Indian who had given Belissari a start back at the arroyo. It was time for a little Greek revenge.

Belissari's first shot split the stock of the Henry and sent both Indian and rifle to the ground. The Apache reached for the rifle, but the horseman fired again and heard the bullet whine off the barrel as the rifle spun in the dirt. Now the Apache was running for cover, but for spite Belissari fired two more rounds at the fleeing Indian's feet. Turning, Belissari fired one more round at the nearest Apache and raced to Poseidon, swinging into the saddle and grabbing the rope that led his mustang herd. In an instant he was dashing through the timbers, laughing at the shouts of the Mescaleros behind him.

He let Poseidon run for a couple of miles, then slowed and eased his way out of the mountains. The Indian ponies would be unridable, he knew, but he decided to play it safe. After letting the horses—and himself—catch their breath, he moved at an easy gate, taking advantage of the moonlight to put some distance between him and the Apaches, just in case.

Sleep would have to wait. He decided to ride all night.

Once out of the mountains, West Texas stretched before him under the moonlight, rolling like heavy seas until coming to the next mountain range. A coyote yipped in the distance, and one of the mustangs snorted. Belissari kicked Poseidon forward and moved in the direction of Fort Davis, careful not to tax his horse or the mustangs he pulled behind him. By the time the Big Dipper showed it to be about two in the morning, he was relaxed but surprisingly not tired.

Picking his way through the next range, he continued, turning toward the Davis Mountains, Fort Davis, Vernon Kaye, and a lot of cash money. By then, the sky was lightening to a dark gray so he dismounted by a small creek and let Poseidon and the other horses graze and drink while he scouted his back trail. He watched quietly for more than a half-hour, but nothing moved as dawn crept forward.

Satisfied, Pete Belissari went back to the creek, drank his fill, and replenished his canteen. He mounted Poseidon and rode toward the Fort Davis road. The skies brightened as he pushed through the mountain passes, humming a few bars of ''Lorena.'' Soon, the orange sun peaked and warmed his entire body. He felt safe, finally. But he heard the sound of hooves behind him, and when he turned, that feeling vanished.

Four horsemen and a riderless mount were heading toward him at a gallop, shouting something but he couldn't make out the words. They were maybe a half-mile behind him, but even from that distance Pete Belissari could make them out as Indians.

He kicked Poseidon into a gallop, pulling his Winchester and slapping the horse's rump with the barrel. ''Come on, boy, run!'' he shouted as he raced down the narrow mountain road. But the horse was tired from carrying him all night. Unless he found shelter fast, he was in for a fight.

Chapter Three

Hannah Scott knelt in the corner of the barn and brushed away hay and dirt until she found the heavy rock, which she pried out with thin fingers, and stared at the hidden cash box. She took a deep breath and opened the box with the key she wore on a leather thong around her neck with her Saint Christopher medallion. Inside were a few pieces of silver and gold, some greenbacks, and the loan agreement she had signed with Rafe Malady two years ago.

After counting the money and scanning the contract, she sighed heavily and carefully returned the items to the metal box, which she slid in the hole and covered. She leaned against the barn wall and buried her face in tired hands. "What did you expect?" she said quietly. "The money to be fruitful and multiply? The due date to change?"

"Mama Hannah?"

The voice startled her, and she jumped while her right hand found the butt of the Navy Colt she had tucked in her apron. The revolver was more than thirty years old—her father had carried it with him during the late war when he served with Hood's First Texas Brigade. It was an antiquated cap-and-ball pistol, .36-caliber, and she hadn't fired it since shooting a rabbit two summers ago. But for the past two months, she had carried it regularly.

Her face flushed when she saw eight-year-old Cynthia, still in her nightclothes, standing in front of her. Hannah left the Colt in her apron and brushed away the loose straw from her gingham dress. "Child," she said softly, "you gave me a start."

"I'm sorry, Mama Hannah," the beautiful, auburn-haired girl replied. "But I'm hungry."

"Come on," Hannah said, and, taking Cynthia's hand in her own, she led her out of the barn and across the yard toward the stone-and-log cabin they called home.

"What would you like for breakfast?" Hannah asked pleasantly.

"Eggs," the girl replied.

"We don't have any eggs."

"I know. The coyotes et all the chickens."

"Ate," Hannah corrected. "Not 'et.' How about some bacon, biscuits, and peaches?"

"Good. I love peaches, Mama Hannah."

Hannah smiled. At first, she had loathed the name "Mama Hannah." After all, she was only twenty-three when she started the orphanage, but gradually she came to like the nickname. Hannah was like a mother to the children she taught, fed, raised, and loved. And she knew what it meant to be alone as a child.

Her mother died in childbirth, and her father left to fight the Yankees when she was only two, sending her to stay with an aunt in Austin. When Hannah was six, a one-armed man in dirty, patched clothes had knocked on the door and left behind a tintype of Hannah's mother, a Bible, a .36-caliber Navy Colt, and word of how Andrew Leslie Scott had died at a place called Sayler's Creek—just days before Robert E. Lee's surrender. Two days later, Hannah Scott found herself in the Travis County orphanage, alone, scared, and treated like a leper by those inside and outside the home.

Hannah vowed then that she would never treat a parentless child like some stray, sick dog, and that she would do everything in her power to see that orphans were loved and taught and given a home—not a prison—to grow up in.

Inside the cabin, Hannah and Cynthia roused the rest of the children and sent them to do their chores, while Hannah fried bacon in the cookshed behind the cabin and Cynthia opened the last two cans of peaches. The table was set when twelve-year-old Christopher, the oldest, came in with a bucket of milk. The kids found their places and bowed their heads, and after Cynthia's prayer, they devoured what little food was on their plates.

"Are we going to have to find a new home?" six-year-old Paco asked.

"Everything will work out," Hannah said.

"Why is that rancher so mean?" cried Angelica,

an overwrought and overweight but sweet girl, ten years old.

"Honey, Mister Malady just wants his money. He's not mean," Hannah replied, though it was a lie. "I owe him money and have to pay him. It's his right."

She sipped coffee, silently fuming, wishing the children would find another topic. Sure, she owed Rafe Malady, or at least his bank, a lot of money—one thousand dollars to be exact—and it was his right to collect. But it wasn't his right to threaten her and the children, to kill their chickens, to run off her live-stock and hired hands. Of course, she could prove none of this—with one exception, and she was too terrified to speak about that.

"Everyone finished?" she asked. And she leaned forward, elbows on the table and chin resting in her right hand, and stared at little Bruce, a sad-eyed boy, maybe nine, who hadn't spoken since a party of Texas Rangers found him on the El Paso road, his parents and two sisters murdered by bandits, and dropped him at Hannah's door fourteen months ago. Of the five children at the orphanage now, Bruce broke her heart the most. He simply looked up at her, unsmiling, and nodded. She tried not to frown and, leaning back in her chair, she finally said, "Well, Christopher, come with me to feed and water the horses. The rest of you, wash the dishes, make your beds, and get out your *McGuffey's Readers.*"

Hannah was walking forward to the well, head bent down, trying to put Bruce, the bank, the orphanage, and Rafe Malady out of her mind. But she couldn't. She had sixty-three dollars and needed a thousand by Monday morning.

And today was Friday.

"Mama Hannah!" Christopher shouted and pointed to the pass on the mountain road. Hannah looked up, stunned. Galloping toward them was a man on horseback, pulling a string of several horses behind him, riding as if the devil himself were in pursuit.

Pete Belissari crested the mountain pass and jerked Poseidon to a stop. One of the mustangs behind him stumbled and almost threw the horseman from his saddle. He glanced back at his pursuers, then scanned the road below. At the foot of the pass stood the old Iverson spread, which had been abandoned and dilapidated the last time he had ridden this road, maybe three years ago. But his keen eyes saw a wisp of smoke coming from the chimney, and two people walking across the yard toward the barn and corral.

Poseidon was lathered with sweat and panting, but Belissari kicked him and the horse took off like a thunderbolt from Zeus, racing down the road toward the ranch. "Come on, boy!" Belissari urged. "Just a little farther!"

Halfway to the ranch, Belissari began shouting at the couple in the yard. "Open the corral! Open the corral! Indians are right behind me!" He was dumbfounded when the two people stood motionless. Blinking sweat from his eyes, he suddenly realized that he was riding to a sandy-haired, lanky boy who could barely be in his teens, and a young, blond woman in a blue-and-white gingham dress and apron.

He reached the yard and leaped from Poseidon's saddle before the horse had completely stopped, ignoring the boy and woman and racing to the corral, pulling the string of mustangs. Quickly he swung open the gate and guided the horses inside. One snorted at the two draft horses in the corral. Belissari whistled and Poseidon trotted behind the mustangs, and the horseman pulled his war bag from the saddle horn as the gray stallion passed by. Then he closed the gate, fastening it shut with the leather strap, and turned toward the boy and woman, glancing at the Indians who were just topping the pass.

The woman, he noticed, was holding a skinny revolver in both hands, the barrel slightly aimed in his direction. She was thin and tan, and the Colt wavered nervously, but her blue eyes flashed with determination. The boy stood at her side, pale, eyes wide.

"Ma'am," Belissari said, gasping for breath and gesturing toward his pursuers. "Indians . . . right behind . . . me. . . . We got to move!"

"Mama Hannah!" the boy shouted, pointing up the road. "He's right!"

She glanced and, lowering the revolver, shouted, "Follow me!" Belissari ran after the two, carrying his Winchester and war bag to the small cabin. The woman held the door open for him, then slammed it shut and barred it as soon as he was inside. Belissari ran to one window in the front, closed the inside shutter, and turned around.

"What in the blazes are all these kids doing here?" he yelled.

Hannah Scott couldn't stop shaking as she placed the revolver on the table. Paco and Angelica were crying in the corner, and Cynthia was hugging both, trying to soothe them, but her own face was white with fright. With his sad eyes, little Bruce sat near them, seeming unable to comprehend the danger.

"Let me help!" Christopher shouted, and the dark, dirty stranger handed him the carbine and a box of shells from the canvas sack he carried.

"You know how to load one?" the man asked.

"Sure," Christopher said, spilling several brass cartridges on the floor as he nervously shoved the bullets into the side of the rifle. The man sat another box of ammunition on the window sill and quickly loaded one shell into the revolver he held deftly in his right hand. He thumbed back the hammer, turned to Hannah, and asked, "Have you any more guns?"

Hannah could only shake her head, pointing at her father's Navy Colt. The man stared at it. "Don't fire that," he said. "It's likely to blow up in your face."

She could only stare at the man, trying to figure him out and her run of bad luck. First Rafe Malady. Now Indians? There hadn't been much Apache trouble since Victorio's death in '80. The stranger wore long, dark hair, uncombed and knotted by the wind, and an adobe-colored hat battered beyond recognition. He was bearded, although it looked as though only his mustache was permanent, with brown, menacing eyes.

His navy flannel shirt was darkened even more by sweat, and he wore Army-issue blue trousers, the thighs and seat reinforced with cowhide, Apache-style moccasins, and a dirty red bandanna.

Horses sounded in the yard, and the children's cries intensified, snapping Hannah out of her daze. "Hush, children, hush," she said. "Everything will be all right." And she picked up the Navy Colt, ignoring the man's warning, and cocked it. She had to adjust the cylinder, which clicked as she lined up the percussion cap with the hammer.

The children's cries had become mere sniffles, and Christopher handed the man his rifle, which he leaned in the corner. "Thanks, son," he said. With grim faces, they waited. The old school clock ticked loudly in the cabin, and the horses outside snorted and whinnied. Footsteps sounded from outside, and then came a voice, in English: "Hello the cabin!"

Pete Belissari's face turned perplexed at the greeting. He glanced at the children, the woman, then at the shutter, which he unfastened and pushed open with the barrel of his Colt, but he kept his body braced against the cabin wall, away from the opening. The woman moved toward the other side of the window, the battered antique pistol in both hands, and stared at Belissari for an answer.

Finally, Belissari took a deep breath and stepped into the light, staring outside at the five tired horses and four men standing in the yard. One of them was dressed in a black broadcloth suit, caked with dust, and gray bell crown hat with a pheasant feather stuck in the hat band.

The man smiled and said in a voice that didn't sound threatening at all:

"Howdy."

Chapter Four

As he stepped onto the porch behind the woman, Pete Belissari felt like a total fool. The four men standing by their horses weren't even armed, and only three were Indians; the man in the suit and hat was white, although his skin had been bronzed by the sun and wind. The Indians' clothes mixed the styles of southern plains warriors and Texas cattlemen. They were Comanche, Belissari guessed, not Apache, and the last hostile Comanches had surrendered years ago.

"I'm Perry Anderson, ma'am, from the Anadarko Agency in the Indian Nations," the man said as he removed his bell crown hat, revealing a bald head. "Sorry, I reckon we gave your husband quite a start back there."

"He's not my husband!" The woman spit out the words like bad water, and she gave Belissari a cold stare before stepping into the yard. "I'm Hannah Scott," she said. "Y'all look tired. Why don't you put the horses in the corral and water them and I'll put some coffee on. There's grain in the barn."

"That's mighty kind of you," Anderson said, and Belissari quickly volunteered to tend the horses. Anything, he thought, to escape the woman's wrath.

The agent and his charges accepted Belissari's offer and the woman's hospitality. After they disappeared into the cabin, Belissari put the five animals in the corral, removed the saddles and bridles, then rubbed them down. When they had cooled, he let them drink. Next, he fed and watered his own horses, unsaddling Poseidon, and brushed and combed the two draft animals of the woman rancher, or whatever she was.

The door opened to the ranch house, and the aroma of coffee knotted Belissari's stomach. Finished, he climbed onto the top rail of the corral and stared at the riderless horse the Comanches and agent had pulled.

It was a magnificent animal, a thoroughbred for sure. The stallion had been at a gallop for miles up and down the mountain passes, and it hardly looked winded. At nineteen hands, it towered over his mustangs, Poseidon, and even the woman's horses. It was blood bay with one white forefoot. *Manoblanca,* the Mexicans called that kind of animal, and he thought of the old saying about horses with white feet:

> Four white feet, just say good-bye
> Three white feet, better be sly
> Two white feet, maybe give him a try
> One white foot, buy, man, buy

"What do you think?"

Belissari turned and looked down at the smiling Perry Anderson, who held a steaming cup of coffee in his right hand.

"He's a beaut," he replied and jumped to the ground. He introduced himself, and after handshakes, both men leaned against the corral and watched the stallion.

"He was clocked at one and a half miles in two minutes, thirty-eight seconds," Anderson said. "That's two seconds and change faster than Buchanan did at the Kentucky Derby this year."

At that, Belissari had to whistle. He wasn't a fan of horse races (well, he had been pleased when Apollo won the Kentucky Derby in '82, but that was just because of the Greek name and the five dollars he won from Vernon Kaye), but that speed was impressive, almost unbelievable.

"Maybe you should take the horse to Louisville next year," Belissari suggested.

The Indian agent laughed. "He's not my horse," he said, jerking his thumb toward the cabin. "The stallion's name is *Ecahcuitzet*—Comanche for Lightning Flash. I wish he were mine, but he belongs to Puha."

The Comanche brave named Niet-tomo—Winter Wind, the agent had translated—was bouncing Paco on his knee, excitedly showing the other children how he had beaten several soldiers at Fort Concho, near San Angelo northeast of here, in a horse race ten days ago. The kids roared with laughter, except Bruce, of course, who stared at the others with his omnipresent grim expression.

Winter Wind was jovial, friendly, with as much energy as a two-year-old. Suddenly, he tossed Paco up, turning him around in midair, and sat him back down on his knee, which bounced up and down like a prancing horse. Paco, now facing his fellow orphans instead of the brave, squealed with delight.

"Now," the young Comanche was saying in perfect English, "I turned around just like Paco here, sitting backward on my horse. So I made faces at the bluecoats. Make a face, Paco!" The six-year-old wagged his ears at the other children. Winter Wind laughed. "The bluecoats were very angry, but they could not catch me. Not when I rode Ecahcuitzet! Make another face, Paco."

Paco did. Angelica stuck out her tongue at him, and Winter Wind and the others laughed. Even Hannah was smiling as she turned to the other two Indians and freshened their coffee.

One of the Indians wore long, gray hair wrapped in otter skins. He was toothless, pockmarked, as old as Methuselah, short and squat with a rounded face crevassed with wrinkles. He held a *McGuffey's Readers* in leathery hands and watched Winter Wind play with the children. Black Bat, he was called, though Hannah couldn't remember how his name was pronounced in Comanche. The ancient medicine man nodded without looking at Hannah and, setting the book aside, he poured more than five teaspoons of sugar into the coffee.

Hannah tried not to grimace. She liked her coffee black, more out of necessity than taste. Sugar was expensive. The other Comanche was tall, with a powerful, hawklike nose and penetrating eyes. He wore heavy leather pants and moccasins, both Comanche style. But his pillow-ticking shirt was store-bought, and he wore a diamond pin stuck in the lapel of his black wool vest. A rock amulet and silk bandanna hung around his neck, and his hat was a steel gray Stetson Boss of the Plains with an eagle feather jutting from the hatband.

Puha, he was called. Comanche for "power," and some people said he was more powerful than any Indian in the Southwest, and most white men. He had been among the last of the Comanche war chiefs to surrender almost ten years ago. Since then, he had dined with ranchers and horse traders, railroad executives and Indian agents, governors and presidents. But all he did in the cabin was stare at the clock on the wall. When it chimed on the hour, he didn't even smile.

The door opened and the Indian agent and stranger entered. Hannah felt her face flush in anger at the imbecile who had scared her and the children half to death. She put the coffeepot on the table and found an extra tin cup for the stranger. Her urge was to fling the scalding liquid in the man's face, but she resisted, and handed him the cup.

"Thanks," he said without looking her in the eye.

"I've got that handbill somewhere," the agent was saying as he fumbled through his saddlebags. "Here!" And he handed the horseman a yellow placard. "Two hundred and fifty dollars to the winner! And what a race it'll be!"

Hannah couldn't resist her curiosity. Peering over the man's shoulder, she read the bold words:

A RACE FOR THE AGES!
Half Past One O'Clock
Sunday, June 1, 1884
The Fort Davis Derby
Six Miles
Top prize: $250!

"Imagine, Mister Belissari," Anderson was saying as Hannah and the horseman read the fine print. "The Belmont Stakes is only one mile and five furlongs. This race will be forty-eight furlongs through open country. And with that prize money, it'll draw a lot of horsemen, though that thirty-dollar entry fee will scare off most local cowboys."

"Town will be booming," the stranger, Belissari, said as he handed the Indian agent the poster. Politely Anderson gave Hannah the notice, and she took it and continued to read.

"And I imagine there'll be a lot of betting going on," Anderson said. "But with Niet-tomo on Ecah-cuitzet, I think Puha has more than a good chance at winning this race. We've already won shorter races at Dallas, Weatherford, and Fort Concho. We got a real good write-up in the *Fort Worth Gazette* too. Maybe you'd like to enter one of your mustangs in this derby."

The man called Belissari laughed, shaking his head. "In a short race, maybe a mustang or a cowboy's quarter horse could give your thoroughbred a race. 'Course, at that distance, six miles, and through rough country, luck and endurance might be more important than horseflesh. I wish you luck.''

''Thanks.'' The man finished his coffee, thanked Hannah, and announced something in guttural Comanche. Winter Wind took Paco off his knee and stood, Black Bat rose, and slowly Puha turned from the school clock. The agent introduced the horseman to the Indians and after a round of handshakes, Anderson looked at Hannah and said, ''Miss Scott, I wish you'd let us repay you for your kindness.''

''It was nothing, Mister Anderson,'' Hannah replied, handing him the placard. He waved his hand and shook his head and told her to keep it. The Indians filed through the door, followed by the children, Belissari, and finally Hannah and the Comanche agent.

They watched from the porch as Black Bat and Winter Wind saddled the horses and led the mounts from the corral. Puha and Anderson mounted, then the other two Indians.

''You say we're ten miles from town?'' Anderson asked, and Hannah nodded.

''Once again,'' the agent continued, ''thank you kindly. Maybe we'll see you in town for Sunday's big race.''

''Yes!'' Winter Wind shouted at the children. ''Come see me ride like the wind.'' And he kicked his horse into a gallop, pulling the blood bay stallion behind him, and disappeared down the road. The other riders followed at a much slower lope, but they too soon rounded the bend and were gone, leaving Hannah Scott alone with her orphans, her problems, and this stranger with the strange name who stood a few yards to her right holding an empty coffee cup like an oaf.

"Children," she said, "back inside. Chris, get them started on their lessons. I'll be inside shortly."

The five children moaned some about doing school-work on such an exciting day but shuffled back into the cabin. When the door had shut, Hannah Scott turned to the stranger, eyes blazing, and barked:

"You must be an *idiot!*"

Pete Belissari knew it was coming, but it was like bracing for a blast of buckshot from a double-barrel shotgun. The woman slammed her fist into his chest, forcing him to step back, and she snapped at him angrily, her ears and face crimson.

"Do you realize how much you scared me and those children? They'll probably have nightmares for a week! The only thing that's keeping me from tearing your head off is that those Indians and the agent were pleasant! But . . ." She barked something that he couldn't understand—nor did he want to. Finally, she had to stop for breath, and Belissari took the opening to plead his case.

"Miss Scott," he said, "you are absolutely right. I'm terribly sorry. I don't know what came over me, except I've been riding all night and had a couple set-tos with some Mescaleros. I'd like to make things up to you somehow."

The woman snorted like an angry mustang. "Yeah," she said, "and just what can you do? Besides scaring kids half to death."

She was somewhat calmer, Belissari noted. He pointed to the roof of the barn. "Roof needs mending,

I see,'' he said. ''I can split some shingles for you, as well as some firewood. Horses, I noticed, could use a good shoeing. I can finish the day here, helping you a bit, then ride on in to Fort Davis tonight.''

''Yeah, you don't have to do me any favors—except maybe ride out of here!'' And she turned abruptly and stormed her way into the cabin. Belissari took pity on the children inside.

He looked at his horses in the corral and thought about riding away. The woman hadn't accepted his offer, but he felt obligated to do something. A wave of exhaustion suddenly enveloped him, and he moped to the well, drew a bucket, and splashed his face. He couldn't just ride away. Sighing, he walked toward the barn to find some horseshoes and nails.

Chapter Five

Old Man Iverson had done a remarkable job when he built the Wild Rose Fork Ranch, Belissari thought as he rested under an oak tree in the gray rocks behind the cookshed after shoeing the horses. The rancher had used the high rock formations for the back of the corral, and the tall palisades of hardened, ancient lava some thirty feet high also protected the ranch yard from northwesterly winds.

Next to the corral stood the wooden barn, crumbling in places now, the rear wall backed up against the northern end of the rocks. Beyond the barn was a dry wash, dotted with yucca and prickly pear, stretching around the rock palisades and leading to a fertile valley of rich grama grass for cattle and horses. The cabin was solidly built of logs and adobe, just south and in front of the corral, and there was the cookshed

35

and an outhouse beyond the cabin, both shaded by the tall rocks and oaks. In the center of the yard stood a well made of limestone, which would provide cool water when the intermittent Limpia Creek was low or dry. That wasn't the case now.

Across the dusty road, the creek flowed—the waters high and turbulent from unseasonal, heavy rains—cutting its way through Limpia Canyon toward Fort Davis.

From any point of the ranch, Belissari had a clear view of Wild Rose Pass just north of the San Antonio–El Paso Road as it stretched past the ranch and rounded a bend a few furlongs to the south, disappearing near a brake of cottonwoods. The ranch was conveniently located, well fortified, shaded, and rich. *If I ever settle down,* Belissari said to himself, *I'd like it to be at a place just like this.*

The cabin's rear door opened, and the children poured out, screaming as if they were fleeing a monster. Belissari smiled, remembering how he and his childhood friends raced out of Mrs. Langston's schoolhouse in Corpus Christi to roughhouse. And later, Belissari and his college friends had raced out of Mister Moore's Latin class to find a poker game or saloon at Louisville.

Hannah Scott walked into the cookshed without speaking, and he heard the clattering of pots and pans as she prepared food for the children, now playing a game with a ball of twine and an oak limb. Belissari put down his book and watched the game. The tall boy, Chris, whacked the make-do ball and sent it sailing toward him. It bounced once, and Belissari caught it with his right hand as the pretty girl skidded to a halt a few feet in front of him, staring as if he were some kind of ogre. Belissari smiled. His niece would be about her age now, he thought, tossing her the ball.

She fumbled with the ball, dropping it and quickly picking it up, and threw it as hard as she could toward the other children. Then she started to run to play, but stopped and looked back at Belissari, who had picked up his book and started to read again. He kept his head down but watched her through the corner of his eye as she ventured toward him. The other children yelled at her, but she waved them off. Finally, Pete Belissari looked up.

The girl stopped suddenly. "Hello," Belissari said. "What are you reading?"

"*The Odyssey* by Homer," he replied. She ventured closer and stared at the open pages. Her nose turned up and she squinted and looked up, perplexed.

"I ain't never seen words like them before."

"It's Greek," he said. His finger found a line. He read, first in Greek, then translated: "The sun rose on the flawless brimming sea." She was impressed, so he repeated, alternating in Greek and English, until he was finished with the verse.

"How did you learn that?" she asked. "I have trouble with our *Readers*."

Belissari laughed, and he noticed the ball game had stopped and the other children were venturing his way. "My mother taught me," he said, "when I was your age. And when I was older, my father made me read the newspapers in English to him, then translate it into Greek. He can't read words too well. But he can read the seas."

The girl looked heartbroken, and Belissari wondered what he had said wrong. "You had a mama and a daddy?" the girl asked, her eyes welling with tears.

"Sure. Still do." And then it hit him like a stallion's kick. The kids were orphans.

Pulling the sourdough biscuits from the oven, Hannah Scott mopped the sweat from her brow with a rag and took a sip of water. Biscuits and potatoes weren't the best meal for growing youngsters, but it was all she had. Suddenly, she noticed the silence. Those children were usually screaming and carrying on like coyotes while she prepared their food, so she pulled off her apron and raced out of the cookshed, expecting them to find them playing by Limpia Creek, which was too dangerous in flood stage, or torturing some rodent.

What she saw surprised her even more.

They sat in a semicircle around the horseman, who was reading from a worn, leather-bound volume. And all of the children, even silent Bruce, were staring at him intently, eyes wide open. She walked closer, dumbfounded, and heard the man called Belissari read: "The Cyclops bellowed and the rock roared around him, and we fell back in fear." He stopped suddenly, noticing her, and the children turned around quickly.

"Mama Hannah!" Cynthia cried. "He's reading us a scary story."

"It's about a one-eyed monster!" Paco added. "It's really good."

Belissari started to rise, shutting the book, but Hannah surprised herself and motioned for him to continue. She had never seen the children so captivated by anything. The man smiled, found his place and continued, "Clawing his face . . ."

With a grunt, Belissari leaned the ladder against the tall barn. He tossed the ball-peen hammer in a can of rusty nails and carried them up, placing them on the edge of the barn's roof, then hurried down to the ground to grab a handful of wood shingles. He was about to start back up when he heard the woman's voice.

She handed him a cup of coffee, and he thanked her and leaned against the ladder, sipping the hot, strong brew as the woman stood silently, her hair and apron blowing in the wind. She still carried the old Navy revolver.

"You've done a lot of work, Mister Bel-B-Belissari." The words were strained, and it wasn't just from pronouncing his Greek surname.

With a shrug, Belissari smiled. "The least I could do, Miss Scott. Call me Pete."

"Pete?"

"Short for Petros."

Silence followed, except for the whistling wind, and Belissari finished his coffee and handed her the empty cup.

"The children," she said, "liked your story. They don't take to strangers quickly, usually." A lot of that, she knew, was because the ranch hands she had hired didn't last long, scared off by Rafe Malady. But she didn't bring that up.

Belissari smiled. "They're great kids."

She took a deep breath and exhaled. "I'd like to

apologize for my actions this morning. I was wrong about you.''

"No ma'am. You were absolutely right, Miss Scott.''

"Hannah," she offered.

He repeated the name. He liked the way it sounded. He liked the way he said it. But he glanced at the ladder and knew he needed to get to work. Instead, however, he asked: "When did you turn the Iverson spread into an orphanage?''

"More than two years ago. I had hoped to be able to run a ranch and orphanage at the same time. You know, raise cattle and horses to bring in enough money for the kids and all.'' She sighed. "But it hasn't worked out too well. You have family? Parents? A, er, wife?''

Belissari nodded, and his polite smile quickly became a frown as he realized how he was answering. "No!" he cried, violently shaking his head and feeling completely stupid. "No wife. I'm not married. My mother and father and sister live in Corpus Christi.''

He told her about his family, how his father had been a fisherman and sailor in Greece before jumping ship near New Orleans in 1851, moving to Galveston and later Corpus Christi, and making his mark and captaincy as a blockade runner during the War Between the States.

Hannah Scott stared at him with the same sad eyes he had seen in Cynthia's face, and he realized that she must be an orphan too, so he quickly changed the subject. They talked about the ranch, mustanging, breaking horses, and the wild roses that grew near the pass. But the conversation slowly died, and Belissari said he had better get to work.

"I'd like you to join us for supper," Hannah blurted out, "if you don't mind." He was about to decline the offer, but she added in a hurried voice, "It's an Apache moon tonight. It'll light up the road all the way to town, which is only ten miles, and the children would love to hear another story. We don't get much Homer read around here." She laughed. "All we have is a Bible and a few *Readers.* I can't promise a spread like you'd get at Buehler's Bakery in town, but we'd love to have you stay."

Belissari smiled. "I can make a pad for you near the children's beds, if you'd like to stay the night too," she added, almost pleading. Her eyes danced, and she smiled, quietly commenting, "You look pretty tired, Mister Be . . . Pete."

He didn't feel tired at the moment, even with a hot sun and an afternoon of working on a crumbling barn roof staring at him. He accepted her offer and watched as she walked back to the cabin. Poseidon snorted from the corral.

"Quiet," Belissari said, and climbed up the ladder.

The hammer connected with Belissari's thumb and he yelped, spitting out nails and shaking his left hand violently. *This is why I work with horses,* he thought. Below, two of the children laughed. It was late afternoon, and the kids were out doing their chores. Angelica was in the corral feeding the horses. Paco and Bruce were gathering wood, Cynthia and Hannah were drawing water from the well, and Chris was sweeping out the cabin.

Belissari picked up the hammer and finished driving a nail. He was on the far end of the barn, near the edge, just above Angelica and the horses. Sucking in air and wiping his forehead, he heard a gasp from Hannah and turned quickly. She was looking at the golden mountain across Limpia Creek, to the right of Wild Rose Pass. Belissari followed her gaze and saw the dust of riders galloping toward the ranch.

"Children!" Hannah shouted. "Get to the house!" She was shaking, her right hand on the revolver's butt, biting her lower lip. Whoever the riders were, she recognized them—and feared them.

Angelica was hurrying toward the corral gate when Belissari called her name. She looked up, and he pointed to his saddle, hanging over the top rail of the corral near the barn. "Do you think you can pull my rifle out of the scabbard and hand it to me?" he asked.

She nodded and raced forward, tugging at the heavy carbine with both hands. Belissari slid down the barn shingles until he was at the edge, dropped to his stomach and stretched his right hand toward the ground. He was still several feet from the ground and wasn't sure if the ten-year-old girl could reach him.

"It's heavy," she said as she pushed the rifle toward him, the barrel sliding against the wooden wall.

"You're doing fine," Belissari praised her. "You can't hurt the rifle. Don't worry." He grunted and stretched his arm more, fingering the cold barrel and jerking it out of her grasp. The carbine flew upward and Belissari caught it firmly and pulled it onto the roof. He rolled over, found his feet and scrambled back toward his hammer, shingles and nails, placing the Winchester out of sight, but within easy reach.

Angelica climbed out of the corral and sprinted toward the cabin. Hannah Scott waited by the well. And Pete Belissari drove another nail, trying to look inconspicuous, counting seven riders and wondering where he could take cover if someone started shooting.

Chapter Six

Hannah Scott stood by the well, biting her lower lip as the riders stormed into the yard and formed a semicircle around her. She forced herself to stand straight, not to cower, and meet each man's stare. In the corner of her eye she saw the mustanger nonchalantly hammering nails. *The fool,* she thought. *Stop that and come down here!* Then her eyes met Rafe Malady's and she turned her anger in the proper direction.

"You're not welcome here, Rafe," she said. "Nor are your men."

Malady sat on a snorting chestnut stallion, flanked by his cowboys. He was a short, barrel-chested man with pale green eyes and white hair. A black Stetson flapped in the wind against his back, held by a latigo string that tugged against his massive neck. Although

44

in his mid-fifties, he was as hard as the Presidio
County terrain and could intimidate, if not best, the
toughest of his riders some thirty years younger.

He wore a green silk bandanna, peach-and-white
pillow-ticking shirt, and green canvas pants stuffed
into tall black boots with a white lone star embla-
zoned on the front. His spurs were black steel, over-
laid with engraved silver, and their jinglebobs added
a musical background to the creaking leather, panting
horses, and Belissari's hammering.

A hand-tooled gun belt and holster was strapped
across Malady's sizable waist, with the long-barreled
Colt's nickel finish and mother-of-pearl grips glisten-
ing in the afternoon sun, but Hannah found herself
studying another weapon. In the rancher's massive
right hand he held a forty-inch leather quirt. Five
months ago, she had watched him whip her hired
hand with the weapon, beating him senseless after he
had refused to be run off her ranch. If Malady's foreman, Buddy Pecos, hadn't pulled his boss away, the
rancher would have killed the young cowboy.

Despite the severity of his injuries, the hand had
ridden out the following morning. Hannah had been
unable to hire any help after that incident. Luckily for
her, the children had been at church that day and
hadn't seen the brutality of it all. She told them that
the cowboy had ridden to see his mother. Maybe he
had.

Belissari's hammer rang out and Malady looked
away, staring at the stranger on the barn roof. The
rancher smiled, slapping his pant leg lightly with the
quirt before he turned back to Hannah. "Another
helper, Hannah?" She felt sick to her stomach as she

watched the man's even but yellow teeth blaze demonically. Rafe Malady, she thought, was beyond evil. He was worse than the devil.

"He's just passing through," Hannah said, hating her weak voice.

"He'd better be." Malady gave the quirt a resounding whack. "Right, Buddy?" The rancher broke out into a hearty laugh.

Long, tall Buddy Pecos, sitting on a roan gelding, did not even crack a smile.

Malady's laugh ceased abruptly and he barked. "You owe me one thousand dollars, Hannah. Do you have it?"

"You know I don't."

"Then I suggest you get you and your kids and your blasted books out of my house. I'll send a wagon over tomorrow to take you and those brats to town."

"You'll do no such thing. I have until Monday to pay you."

The rancher leaned forward in his saddle until he was almost in her face but she refused to back away. His breath smelled of pipe tobacco and rye, rancid and sour. "Where," he whispered, "do you think you're going to get that kind of money over a weekend? You've had almost two years to come up with it, and you ain't got squat."

"Thanks to you. But I'm not licked yet, you heartless pig."

The leather whip exploded again as Malady shot upright in his saddle, his face burning. "By thunder, I'll show you!" He unleashed the quirt and Hannah pulled the Navy pistol and pointed it at the rancher's face. She pulled back the hammer with trembling hands.

"No one!" Malady boomed. "No one pulls a gun on me!" He jerked his right arm above his head, ready to strike Hannah with his whip, unable to believe that she would actually pull the trigger. His men stared at them in disbelief, except for Buddy Pecos, who sat unconcerned, his one good eye dead.

A voice thundered, "Hey, fat man!" Everyone turned toward Belissari on the barn. He was holding his Winchester, sliding down the wood-shingled roof.

The shingles bit into Pete Belissari's rear end as he slid forward, gaining speed. He held the carbine with both hands, finger against the trigger and stock against his shoulder as he bounced down the roof. Suddenly, the horseman realized that if he didn't stop, he was going over the edge, onto the ground and probably breaking his legs, possibly his neck. That wouldn't help Hannah, and definitely wouldn't cause the seven riders to fear him. He needed to put out his hands to stop his tumble, but he couldn't lower the Winchester. That would give the riders time to draw their weapons—and maybe kill him.

With his feet, he dug in against the roof, the wood and nails biting through the soles of the soft leather moccasins. At the same time, he leaned back and put more weight onto his butt. His descent slowed and he regained control, stopping at the edge of the roof. From below, he thought, it probably looked as if he had planned it that way.

"Put it down," Belissari said evenly, keeping the Winchester planted against his shoulder, unflinching. "Now."

The fat man lowered the whip but he wasn't pleased. His face was crimson, his ears even darker, and with his white hair he reminded Belissari of a snow-capped volcano about to erupt.

"You're making a big mistake, mister," the man said.

"Maybe."

"You shouldn't stick your nose in something that ain't your affair."

"Maybe," Belissari repeated.

The rancher exploded with a deluge of furious oaths. *He's not tall but he sure isn't short on temper,* Belissari thought as the rancher slapped the quirt against his horse, which started dancing and caused the other riders to begin shifting uncomfortably in their saddles, trying to steady their own mounts. The man screeched and bellowed until he should have been exhausted, then calmed his jumpy chestnut and kept yelling at Belissari.

"You start the ball here and you'll rue the day!" the rancher shouted. "You got a name, stranger?"

That's a rude question, Belissari thought. In western etiquette, one didn't ask another man's name. Belissari grinned.

"Maybe," he said, enjoying himself as the rancher flew into another rage.

"This woman is squatting on my land. I'm evicting her."

Belissari changed his vocabulary. "Nope," he said.

"Pecos!" the rancher shouted and Belissari's smile vanished. *Hope I haven't gone too far,* he said to himself.

Until that moment, Hannah had not noticed the

heavy Sharps rifle cradled in Buddy Pecos' arms across his lap. It was a single-shot rifle but she had seen Pecos shoot before. One round was all he usually needed to bring down a mountain lion, deer, or— many said—a man. Folks claimed that he had served as a sharpshooter for the Confederacy, then had made a brief career as buffalo hunter and bounty hunter before joining up with Malady's outfit.

All he had to do was swing down from his horse, use the animal as a shield and fire at Belissari, who was in the open at the edge of the roof. She remembered the Navy revolver in her hands and was turning the barrel away from Malady and toward the foreman when she heard Belissari's voice again.

"Hey, Cyclops! You like getting paid?"

Belissari had noticed the Sharps, and the man called Pecos. He was rail-thin, maybe six-foot-five in his stocking feet, and he was wearing high-heeled boots. A gray slouch hat, so worn, faded, and covered with dust that it was almost white, covered his head. His hair was light brown, graying, thinning but long. But it was his face that caught your eye.

Pecos's oft-broken nose resembled a hawk's beak, and a large brown leather patch covered his right eye. His other eye was pale, a lifeless blue, Belissari guessed from the distance. A bulge of tobacco was knotted on his left cheek and he spit out a long stream of black juice, unconcerned about the remnants that dripped down his stubbled chin. Underneath the eye patch were several white scars and a dark, almost black spot where, Belissari guessed, gunpowder had been embedded under the skin. On his other cheek stretched a massive scar from the bridge of his nose, forking like a river toward the corner of his twisted mouth and mangled ear. Hair refused to grow over the scars, and the face—the one eye—gave him the appearance of a monster.

Buddy Pecos made no effort to move. His rifle remained cradled, his feet in the stirrups. He didn't speak but kept his good eye trained on Belissari, ignoring the wrath of his boss.

"Pecos! *I'm* paying you. You take orders from me—"

"Mister Malady," the tall, deformed man finally said in a deep Southern drawl, "that feller ain't aimin' his Winchester at me. His sights ain't budged off you."

Malady's head jerked up. Sure enough, the stranger on the roof was aiming at him, ignoring the other six men. Malady had played enough poker to know the man wasn't bluffing. He glanced at Hannah, who had turned her pistol back on him, and nervously tapped his pant leg with the whip again.

"It ain't over," he told her softly.

"Get off my land!"

Malady looked back at the man on the barn roof. "Stranger, you just bit off more than you can chew. This witch owes me one thousand dollars by Monday, else I'm foreclosing on this ranch. And after I cart her off, I'm gonna teach you a thing about manners."

"Maybe," Belissari said, then added, "but I have my doubts. I just might know where Miss Scott can find that thousand dollars."

Malady laughed, but it was uncertain. "You're a worthless saddle tramp. You ain't got that kind of cash, and them horses in the corral ain't gonna bring no thousand dollars.''

''We'll find out Monday, won't we?'' Belissari inhaled and exhaled, keeping his rifle trained on the rancher. The man was short and solid, not what you would think of as a horseman, but Belissari had to respect the way he forked a horse. And the chestnut he rode was a fine animal.

''You and your riders are well mounted,'' Belissari said. ''Now let's see if you can't keep 'em at a high lope until y'all disappear over that ridge. If you make good time, I might be inclined not to shoot. But if anyone stops, I'll drop him.''

Malady pointed a short, stubby finger at him. ''You'll pay for this, mister.''

Belissari pulled the trigger.

The shot echoed across the hills and kicked up dust in front of Malady's horse, which almost pitched the rancher onto the ground. Malady dropped the quirt and pulled on the saddle horn until the animal quit bucking, then he gathered his reins and raked the horse's sides with his spurs, galloping out of the yard and followed by his men.

Except Buddy Pecos.

The foreman stared at Belissari for a few moments without speaking, watching the mustanger jack another shell into the Winchester's chamber. *He's sizing me up,* Belissari thought. Hannah trained her Navy .36 at Pecos but he ignored her. Slowly he lifted the heavy Sharps and shoved it into his saddle scabbard. Then he leisurely turned around, tipped his battered hat at Hannah, and said, ''Ma'am,'' then followed Malady and his men at a deliberate pace.

Belissari had to admire the rider. He was ugly as all get-out but he had style, class . . . and courage. But Pete shifted his Winchester toward the foreman and didn't lower the rifle until he and the other men had disappeared over the mountains.

Chapter Seven

"It's not over," Hannah said softly. "Not by a long shot."

The wind had carried the dust toward Fort Davis after Buddy Pecos followed the last of Malady's riders over the northeastern peak. Belissari was well aware that a man with a Sharps "Big Fifty" could kill him from that distance yet somehow he believed that wasn't the one-eyed gunman's style. But just to be on the safe side, he told Hannah, "I think we should go inside."

She didn't seem to hear him. Staring into the distance, eyes blank, she tried to stick the Navy into her apron but missed twice. Belissari realized that *the Colt was still cocked* and moved quickly toward her. She angrily jabbed the revolver again, fuming, and

53

Belissari took her hand firmly and pried the gun from her grip.

"Easy," he said. "You could shoot yourself." He squeezed the trigger until it clicked slightly, then gently lowered the hammer with his thumb, adjusting the loose cylinder until it rested on an unloaded chamber. Almost immediately, he dropped the revolver onto the dirt as well as his Winchester and reached for her, catching her before she fell backward in a faint. She was light in his arms as he drew her close, holding his breath until her eyes regained their focus and she almost leaped out of his grasp, blazing in anger and embarrassment, smoothing her blouse and apron.

"I hate that!" she said bitterly. He wasn't sure what she meant, so he kept silent. "I hate to faint! It's so weak!" She bent forward and grabbed the antiquated pistol, shoving it successfully into her apron this time and turning toward the house. Just as quickly, she stopped and turned back toward the horseman.

"I'm sorry," she apologized. "I didn't mean to take it out on you."

Belissari shrugged. "I'll meet you inside," he said. He picked up the Winchester, made sure the barrel and mechanisms were fine and walked to the barn. He had draped his gun belt and Colt across the saddle before beginning the chores. Now he fed cartridges into the shell belt until it was full and buckled it on. He also found a box of .44–40s for the carbine. Like she said: It's not over.

Glancing at the peak across Limpia Creek, Belissari headed toward the cabin.

Inside, the children were nervously excited, a cacophony of voices bouncing off the adobe and log walls. "What happened? We heard a gunshot!" "We were scared." "Is everything all right?" "Who shot the gun?" "Is it over?" "Is Mister Belissari shot?"

Pete Belissari walked into the cabin, placing the Winchester in the corner. "Mister Belissari is fine," Hannah said, glancing at the horseman. "Everything's all right now. There was just a little misunderstanding."

"Oh, I'll bet," the boy named Chris said—quite cynically for a twelve-year-old, Belissari thought, but he had to smile.

"I wanted to help!" the boy named Paco shouted, stabbing his toy spear at Belissari. "Just like them Greeks and that monster man!"

Hannah clapped her hands, and silence ensued. "Let's get supper started. Mister Belissari is our guest and I promised him a feast for a king."

Belissari sat on an overturned box on the cabin's small porch. The sun was sinking and the wind had died, turning the evening pleasant. Inside the cabin, the children were preparing supper. Across from him stood Hannah. He had left the carbine inside, but the Colt hung heavily and comfortably on his right hip. In his right hand was a cup of coffee. In his left was the paperwork to the agreement Hannah had signed with the rancher Rafe Malady.

He had asked to see the paper, hoping to find a loophole or some way he could help without having to come up with a thousand dollars, which he didn't have anyway. She went to the barn and returned in a few minutes with documents full of legalese. "It's all

Greek to me,'' he told the children and Hannah. After they sighed, he smiled and added, ''But I read and write Greek.''

It was one of his favorite jokes and he never tired of using it.

He pored over the papers, occasionally glancing at Hannah. It was hard to concentrate with her there but he was disciplined. Pete Belissari wasn't a lawyer but he could tell that the contract was wound tighter than a two-dollar watch. One thousand dollars. Payable on Monday. Or else.

Sighing, he returned the document to Hannah. She looked hopefully at him, then slowly shook her head. ''I figured as much,'' she said.

''How much money do you have?''

She sniffed. ''Sixty-three dollars.''

Belissari exhaled. ''I'll sell the horses to the Army for six hundred and seventy-five dollars. That's close. I can wire my father in Corpus Christi—''

''It won't work. Rafe Malady wants one thousand dollars in cash in his hand Monday or else. Your father couldn't wire the money by then, and even if he could, Malady wouldn't allow it. This is his town, Pete. I even thought about entering that horse race for two hundred and fifty. Even with that, we'd still be short. Besides, this is my problem. You've done enough. I won't let you put up your own money.''

Belissari held up his hand in protest. ''It's not charity, Miss . . . Hannah. I'm a horseman and I could use a place to corral my mustangs. Your location is perfect. We'd be doing each other a favor.''

Hannah smiled. ''Except it won't work. You don't have the money. I don't have the time.''

Silence followed; the coffee turned cold. "How'd you come to be indebted to a man like this Rafe Malady?" the mustanger finally asked.

Hannah smiled again. "Bad luck." She let out a sigh that seemed heartbreaking and began her story.

"I bought this place underneath Malady's nose. He was out of town, visiting his brother I think, and I got it at a tax sale of lands. Seems like everyone but me knew not to bid on it. That was two years ago.

"Rafe was friendly at first. He offered me money for the land—his ranch is over the ridge; we're neighbors. But I stood my ground, told him my plans for an orphanage. He seemed to accept that, even loaned me money to fix up the place—and it sure needed that. That was six months later, and I accepted. I figured I could raise the money with cattle and donations in eighteen months.

"And there were no problems until about a year ago. Then Mister Malady turned nasty. Poisoned wells. Run off stock. Killed my chickens. He scared off anyone I hired and beat a poor boy almost to death who wouldn't scare so easily. I haven't had any hired hands since."

"What about the law?"

"Rafe Malady's the law here. Besides, no one would believe me over him. He's a rich, respected rancher. His brother is a lawyer—he drew up this contract—and owns a few hotels in Marfa, Fort Stockton. Some sad story, huh?"

She's beautiful, Belissari thought. He shook himself out of his daze, aware that he had been staring at her the whole time, and nodded, rising slowly. She was near him, so close that he could smell the flour on her, the baking powder, the rose perfume. She stuck the papers in her apron near the omnipresent Colt Navy but she didn't back away, looking up at him with wonderful blue eyes.

"We're going to fix this thing," he said quietly. "I don't know how, but it's going to work out."

She smiled. "I can't believe how wrong I was about you," she said, almost giggling. "I can't believe I almost ran you out of our lives. You know, I could have shot you this morning?"

Belissari pointed to her Colt. "Not with that old thing."

Her laughter filled the night, and he put his arms around her waist and drew her close. She closed her eyes and he bent forward, opening his mouth as his heart raced and he heard the door swing open and Angelica scream, "Supper's ready!"

Hannah pulled away, wiping away her smile as she shot into a ramrod position and stared at the chubby ten-year-old. "Very good," she said, struggling with the words. "Let's eat." She glanced back at Belissari, shrugging, and walked inside.

Pete Belissari poured the cold coffee on the ground and followed, grumbling, "I hate kids."

"Tell us about the Greek gods!" Paco said after supper, brandishing his toy spear. Belissari pushed himself away from the table. Cynthia, the eight-year-old, shouted, "No! Read to us from that fancy book!" Belissari nodded toward his leather volume and two of the children raced to bring it.

"I think the Greek gods could hold nothing to

you," he said. "In fact, in Greece folks probably would think you were gods in disguise."

He lifted the always-silent Bruce on his knee and ruffled his hair. "Bruce, with these dark eyes and hair. I'd say he was Apollo, taking everything in. Apollo was the god of law." He lowered Bruce, hoping for a reaction, but got only silence.

"I want to be Mars!" Paco shouted. "He's the god of war! A boy at church told me that."

Belissari frowned. "Roman god, Paco. We weren't too keen on Roman mythology in my family. We'll make you Ares, the *Greek* god of war."

"What about me?" Angelica said as she handed Belissari the book of Homer. "Did them Greeks have girl gods?"

"They were called goddesses, honey," Hannah said, and Belissari nodded.

"Yes ma'am, and you'd be Hera. She had red hair and green eyes just like yours. Hera means *lady* in Greek. Chris, being the oldest and the ruler of this roost, he'd be Zeus, the ruler-father, god of lightning. And you"—he pushed a strand of hair out of Cynthia's face—"you'd be Artemis. She was beautiful, just like you, the goddess of the hunt, and she sometimes went by the name of Cynthia."

"And Mama Hannah?" Cynthia said.

The horseman's and Hannah's eyes met, and both smiled. "I don't think," he said, "that any goddess could compare to Mama Hannah."

Hannah laughed. "I see the Greeks are high on flattery, Mister Belissari."

"Read!" the children shouted in unison, and Paco turned open the book and pointed. "Read this!"

Belissari spoke in Greek, then translated: "How welcome the word 'bed' came to his ears! Now, then, Odysseus laid him down and slept. . . ."

He stopped abruptly as he was trampled by exhaustion. The words seemed to strike a nerve in his brain reminding him of the last time he had slept. "Wow," he said quietly and couldn't suppress a yawn. "Gods and goddesses, I'm suddenly all tuckered out."

Hannah clapped her hands. "All right, children. We'll see Mister Belissari off tomorrow morning. Let's all get ready for bed."

Belissari stumbled to the pallet in the corner of the cabin, guided by Hannah Scott. He unbuckled the gun belt and sagged to the covers, mumbling something incomprehensible. Hannah just laughed, seeming to forget her problems.

"Sleep well, Pete," she said, brushing a bang off his forehead. She had just stood up when the first bullet shattered a window.

Chapter Eight

A heavy slug shattered the glass and knocked open an unfastened shutter. The children screamed as another bullet sang off an inside wall. Hannah dropped to the floor, covering her head as glass rained over her, screaming, "Children! Stay down! Get under your beds!" Her voice was lost under a deafening fusillade of gunfire, hard thuds pounding against the wall and closed shutters and the repeated zing of a ricochet.

Belissari was wide awake as he rapidly crawled across the floor, the broken glass biting into his left hand and knees. Quickly he slid up the wall, fired his Colt once, and slammed the shutter, rapidly securing it with a rawhide thong and dropping back down as several bullets tore through the wood shutter and sent splinters flying everywhere.

Within seconds he had bolted the door, shoved the Colt in his waistband and picked up the Winchester. He looked for Hannah, who was moving quickly now, blowing out the lantern and cocking her Navy Colt. She lunged toward Belissari and slid against the wall, panting heavily.

In the darkness the bullets continued to sing.

"Is everyone all right?" Hannah shouted.

"Yes Mama Hannah," a girl whimpered.

"What's happening?" Paco screamed.

"Just stay down!" Hannah yelled.

A bullet bounced off the wall and shattered a ceramic pitcher, showering the table with water. Belissari knelt beside Hannah and whispered, "We have to get these kids out of here. All of us. They keep this fire up, we'll be riddled with bullets." His remarks were punctuated by several whines and thumps as a heavy lead bullet bounced across the room, kicking up a puff of dust over their heads as it finally lodged in the adobe.

"The back door," Hannah said, gasping. "Hide in the rocks." She raised her voice and shouted instructions to Chris.

"Make sure they get there," Belissari said. He straightened, removed the bar from the door, and rushed outside, firing the Winchester carbine from the hip.

The moon was large and full, casting a white glow on the ranch yard as bright as dawn. In West Texas, it was known as an Apache moon, raiding season for the Indians. But the riders attacking the Wild Rose Fork Ranch were not Apaches. They were white men—and Belissari had a pretty good idea whom they worked for.

Belissari crouched behind an oak column on the porch and fired again. He could see several riders milling by the corral, raising dust, the white smoke pouring from rifles and six-shooters. He fired twice more, hoping to draw their attention and provide cover for Hannah and the orphans as they made their way to the hiding place in the rocks.

His shots were answered by the thunder of a heavy rifle, the bullet smacking inches above his head. A few other shots, not as well aimed, hit the ground and rafters. He was parched. He sucked in air, looked around, and furiously cocked the carbine.

The night smelled of sulfur, dust, and wood smoke. It was only then that Belissari saw the orange glow coming from inside the barn.

The riders had set the barn on fire!

''Get them horses!'' someone shouted and Belissari fired again as he saw a man dismount to open the corral gate. He had to duck and flatten himself on the porch as his gunshot was answered by a cannonade of rifle fire, splintering the wood column and overturned crate nearby.

He rolled onto his back, jacking another shell into the carbine, its barrel already hot to the touch, and saw Hannah run outside and take cover beside the opposite oak column. She raised the Navy Colt and before Belissari could shout ''No!'' she pulled the trigger.

The cap-and-ball pistol exploded in her hand, a muffled concussion that peppered Belissari with grease, and Hannah screamed and was sent reeling against the wall. Belissari rocked himself to his feet, fired once, and dived toward the injured woman. She was on her knees, biting her lips hard, squeezing an already swelling right hand as if she were trying to keep her fingers from falling off.

A bullet clipped a lock of Belissari's hair and he fell forward, covering the woman with his body. He rolled off after the latest round of fire and pulled Hannah inside the cabin.

"Let me see!" he shouted but Hannah, her eyes filled with tears, stubbornly shook her head.

Belissari loosened her grip. By the light of the moon he could see that she hadn't lost any fingers, but her hand was black and blue and her trigger finger and thumb were torn by shrapnel. He untied his bandanna and wrapped it around her hand.

"You'll be all right," he said, not even considering scolding her for ignoring his persistent warnings about trying to shoot that piece of junk. He pulled his Colt from the holster and placed it on her lap. She would have to use her left hand but he dared not leave her unarmed in case he were killed. "Stay here," he said and dived outside again.

Black smoke and orange flames leaped from the barn and Belissari saw the riders stampeding his horses out of the yard and toward Wild Rose Pass. He yelled, "Poseidon!" at the top of his lungs and whistled shrilly. He breathed easier when he saw the gray horse pull out of the panicking herd and gallop toward him.

"Kill that hoss!" someone shouted and a rider reined up short and turned, raising a rifle. Belissari's Winchester was pressed against his shoulder in a flash. He found the man in his sights and squeezed the trigger.

The man reeled in the saddle and pitched forward as his horse did a side dance. He dropped his weapon and clung to the animal's neck as Poseidon loped into the yard. Another rider spurred back toward the wounded man, gathered the loose reins, and galloped after the other riders and stolen horse herd, pulling his wounded comrade behind him.

Poseidon stopped in front of Belissari but there was no time for praise. The inferno that once was the barn intensified. Belissari raced toward the corral, shielding his face with his left hand. He gathered his saddle and tack and stumbled toward the house. He dropped it in the middle of the yard when he saw Hannah racing from the house toward the inferno.

Belissari darted toward her, leaped out, and tackled her just yards from the burning barn. The heat and smoke burned his lungs and singed his hair. He gasped and shouted, "What are you doing?"

"My money!" she screamed hysterically. "The money's in the barn!"

He jerked her to her feet and pulled her toward the well. "Sixty-three dollars ain't worth dying for!" he shouted. He shook her. "The money's gone! We have to save the house! Do you understand?"

She nodded.

"Kids!" he shrieked. "Paco! Chris! Everyone to the well!"

The children rounded the corner, eyes wide with fright, most of them crying. "Bucket brigade!" Belissari barked. "Forget the barn. Soak the house! The roof especially!"

Belissari drew a bucket of water, poured it into another bucket, and watched as Angelica passed it to Bruce, who passed it to Paco. The six-year-old stumbled, sloshing water left and right, as he handed the heavy bucket to Cynthia. She in turn passed it to Chris, who heaved the water onto the cabin's roof. Chris handed the empty bucket to Hannah and she carried it hurriedly to Belissari in her good hand. Belissari drew another load of water, then found an empty bucket beside the well. "Two buckets!" he shouted. "We'll use two buckets. Faster!"

He lost track of time as he drew and poured water into the two buckets, no longer watching the line of young firefighters. The fire roared and his clothes were hot, maybe even smoking. Belissari realized the potential danger and he stopped the line to soak everyone's clothes with buckets of water, first the children's, then Hannah's, finally his own. The wet clothes and hair cooled him for a minute but relief didn't last long. They had barely resumed the bucket brigade when heavy smoke began hovering over them like fog, causing them to cough and wheeze.

"Help us, Apollo!" Belissari said. The smoke would kill them all, burning their eyes and throats, filling their lungs. "Help us, God!" he prayed. "Help us."

The wind suddenly picked up and blew the smoke away, lifting the smoke and soot that had blackened their faces, clothes, and spirits. Belissari sucked in hot air and filled another bucket. He coughed violently, trying to rid his insides of the thick smoke, wiped his eyes, and lowered the bucket into the well. "Faster," he said, wheezing. "Faster."

Trees and shrubs near the barn caught fire but the recent heavy rains had soaked the land and the blaze refused to spread farther although the massive boulders smoked from the heat. The roof to the barn collapsed, showering the air with sparks and embers, and Poseidon danced nervously, untethered. "Easy, boy," Belissari said, glancing at the gray horse and the burning barn. He briefly thought about all of the wasted work he had done repairing the shingles but his mind quickly refocused on the task at hand as he filled another bucket of water.

Exhausted, Bruce and Paco crumpled in the line but the other children left them there, filling in the gaps, stepping over their bodies to pass the buckets of water, neither complaining nor panicking, just doing what had to be done. *They're good children,* Belissari said to himself. But he had known that already.

The north wall to the barn folded into the corral and the rest of the barn collapsed in an explosion of fire and smoke, shooting sparks toward the brilliant moon as if it were the Fourth of July.

Wheezing, crying, Cynthia finally sank onto her knees, haggard-looking with red eyes and a black face. Angelica stopped moving. Chris wearily poured a bucket onto the roof and looked at Hannah and Belissari, who looked at the ruins of the barn.

"I think the house is safe," Belissari said. His voice, chapped and dry from smoke, heat and exhaustion, surprised him and he drew another bucket, cupped his hands, and drank. Hannah and Chris also gulped thirstily. He motioned to the other children, and Chris took the bucket toward Angelica.

Belissari's hands were blistered from the heat and

hoisting the rope but he ignored the injuries and drew another bucket. This one he took toward the barn. He was so tired that he almost dragged the bucket, sloshing water onto the hot ground, and he emptied the container onto the dying fire of what once had been a giant barn.

The fire sizzled and popped, and mechanically, almost dreamlike, Belissari walked back toward the well, got more water, and forced himself toward the fire. This time he was followed by Chris and Hannah, each carrying buckets of water. They kept it up until the ashes and blackened timber were smoking. Poseidon snorted. It was only then that Belissari noticed the graying in the eastern horizon that meant dawn.

Chapter Nine

"Who would do that?" Angelica said between sobs. "Who would shoot at us? Who would burn down our barn?"

"Was it Apaches?" Paco screeched. "I should have grabbed my spear."

Belissari was finishing dressing Hannah's injured right hand. It was numb and her wrist was probably sprained but he had cleaned the bloody finger and thumb, applied salve to it generously, and wrapped it in his red bandanna.

"This will have to hold till Fort Davis," he said softly. "Think you can walk that far?"

She nodded and Belissari continued. "Get a doctor to look at it, if not in town, then head to the fort and tell Captain Vernon Kaye that I sent you. Report this to the sheriff—"

"He won't do anything," Hannah said bitterly. "He's probably not even in town."

"Report it anyway."

"Did you see who they were?" Cynthia asked.

"I didn't have to," Belissari replied drily, more to Hannah than to the girl.

He moved quickly, scrubbing the black and grime off the children's faces with well water, then picking the glass shards from his hand and washing his other cuts. He reeked, and his own face remained darkened from the fire, the whites of his eyes inflamed from smoke, dirt, no sleep, and boiling anger.

"Chris," Belissari said, "you're going to have to make sure Hannah and the little ones get to Fort Davis all right. Maybe people in town saw the fire last night and are on their way. Maybe not. It's ten miles. Can you handle that?"

"Yes sir," the boy said grimly.

"What about me?" Paco shouted. "I got a spear. And I'm Ares, the god of war. I can help!"

Belissari controlled his urge to snap at the youth. The boy's shrill voice aggravated Belissari's already frayed nerves. He calmed himself, however, exhaled, and forced a smile. "That's right, Paco. You take that spear and watch for snakes."

"Yes, sir!"

His hand clutched the butt of his Colt revolver and he slowly withdrew it from the leather holster, spinning the short barrel toward him and flicking his wrist so that the butt was extended toward Chris.

"You know how to use this?" Belissari asked the boy.

"Yes, sir," Chris replied, "but I think you'd better keep it."

At that moment, Petros Belissari no longer thought of Chris as a twelve-year-old boy. He was a young adult, well on his way to manhood. He nodded and holstered the Colt. His eyes met Hannah's and locked, but neither spoke for a minute.

"Come to town with us!" Angelica begged, but Belissari shook his head sadly.

"I've got to get my horses back," he said flatly. But that wasn't the reason he was going, six hundred and seventy-five dollars or not.

"Children!" Hannah said. "Get inside and gather some food, canteens, and some clothes. We'll see if the Reverend Cox will put us up for a while. It isn't safe here anymore."

Sobbing, the children walked into the cabin, leaving Hannah and the horseman alone in the cool morning.

"Malady won't bring your horses to his ranch," she said, "not stolen stock. He's not that stupid."

"I know, but I've got a pretty fair idea of where he'd hide them."

Her voice rose. "Why don't you come to town, get help there? You don't have to go after them alone!"

Shaking his head, Belissari replied, "Like you said, it's Rafe Malady's town. I couldn't get help in Fort Davis."

"But the Army, your friend the captain—"

"It's not an Army matter."

She closed her eyes, accepting his resolve. He stepped toward her and her eyes opened. He pushed her damp bangs from her forehead and tried to think of something to say but the words refused to come. Poseidon snorted and the children filed out of the house excitedly. "We're ready, Mama Hannah," Cynthia said.

Hannah reached out with her left hand and pressed her fingers gently on the horseman's lips. "Be careful," she said and turned toward the children.

"I'll see y'all in town this afternoon," Belissari shouted lamely, watching them file down the road and disappear around the bend of cottonwood trees. He listened for their voices until he had to strain his ears, then he turned and saddled Poseidon. He reloaded the revolver and carbine, set his hat on his head, and swung into the saddle.

He kicked Poseidon into a gallop and burned his way down the San Antonio–El Paso Road, heading northeast over Wild Rose Pass and toward Fort Stockton. There was no need to try and follow the tracks of the stolen horse herd. Pete Belissari knew exactly where he was going. It had been a long time since he had paid a visit to Roland Kibbee's trading post.

A few miles down the pass, he turned off the road at a curve and headed east. Poseidon's hooves splashed in the rapidly flowing Limpia Creek, its banks lined with Emory oak, but the water was not deep at the crossing and they made it across without incident. A rugged peak stood in front of him, a barren expanse of rock jutting almost six thousand feet into the blue sky. Patches of yucca, one-seed juniper, and tree cholla surrounded the summit.

Untrampled grama grass swayed in the morning breeze. The thieves hadn't taken the stolen horses this way but that didn't matter to Belissari. In fact, it was better this way.

He would have to pick his way around the base of the dark mountain, forcing his way through any brambles or rock slides until he came to the easternmost side. An intermittent creek flowed there, cutting a canyon that would provide a road north, protecting him from being seen by anyone at Roland Kibbee's—providing that Rafe Malady hadn't posted a man there.

Once in the canyon, he would ride easily north, circle around another ridge, and head toward the trading post at the bottom of a rise, surrounded by catclaw and juniper in Horse Thief Canyon. The canyon was well named, Belissari thought.

Poseidon cautiously maneuvered his way around the peak, snorting from the effort as loose stones were overturned and the iron shoes occasionally clanged on hard rock. Belissari patted the gray steed's neck and praised him. A brief, carpeted path provided some relief but then Belissari had to dismount and stumble forward across a pile of boulders and debris ten feet high that blocked the way.

Between curses and grunts, he pulled hard on the reins and Poseidon responded, groping his way over the rocks, raising dust and causing minor rock slides until at last, exhausted, man and horse tumbled onto the other side.

Belissari felt his sweat-soaked shirt sticking on his back and slaked his thirst with water from his canteen. He led Poseidon inside the narrow canyon and found the swift-current stream in flood stage. Poseidon drank for a minute, then Belissari swung into the saddle.

The dark, steep canyon walls loomed menacingly over him, and though it was cooler, sweat still poured from his body. He slowly withdrew the Winchester, cocked it, and cringed as its metallic sound was magnified in the canyon. Scanning the rocks, he saw no one but he felt a tightening in his stomach and wondered if he had made a grave mistake.

This canyon was a good shortcut to Kibbee's. But it also was a death trap.

Running water splashed over rocks, and Belissari noticed another giant rock slide in front of him. The other bank was clear and he would have to cross the creek, but in the water he would be an easy target. He had no other choice. Poseidon couldn't climb over that barrier so he eased the gray horse into the swift stream.

The horse whinnied but moved forward sluggishly. The creek was deeper than Belissari had imagined and he felt icy water soak his moccasins. He tightened the grip on the reins, kicking Poseidon lightly. The horse lost its footing for a second, almost spilling Belissari, but Poseidon quickly recovered and moved faster toward the bank.

Belissari pulled the Winchester up toward his chest and glanced behind him. A gunshot thundered and he felt his hands ring and go numb as the Winchester flew apart with a whine and catapulted him into the cold water. He went under, then came up quickly, gasping. The current took him downstream and he swallowed more water. Echoes of the rifle shot boomed throughout the canyon, sounding as if he were in the midst of a major battle.

He saw the spray of water in front of him and heard

another shot and more echoes. Kicking forward, he went under and tried to swim toward the bank but his head slammed into a sharp rock and he groaned, swallowing mouthfuls of the creek water, which forced him to surface and gasp for air. He clawed his way to shallow water, his hands still ringing. Coughing, he stumbled forward. Blood streamed from his left temple down his cheek. Water and dirt almost blinded him.

Poseidon stood patiently on the banks, unflinching despite the reverberating gunshots, but the horse was some thirty yards from him and another bullet splashed between his legs. As his hands regained their feeling, he slapped his holster and drew the Colt. Ahead of him stood a giant boulder partly in the water and shore, and he lunged for it, planting himself against its side as a bullet zipped past his right ear.

Stupid! Belissari said to himself, pounding his right calf with the butt of his Colt. *Penned like a mustang!* The rifle above him roared again and spanged across his makeshift fort. There was only one gunman, Belissari realized, but he was well positioned with a high-powered, long-range weapon. A Sharps "Big Fifty," he figured, and the thought made him sick. *Buddy Pecos!*

Pete Belissari was in a bind. His head wound slowly clotted and he gathered air and energy. His soaking hat, held in place by the stampede string, hung over his wet, heaving chest. The rest of his clothes were heavy, covered with wet sand and dead grass. He dried the Colt .45 as best he could on his shirt, hoping that the brass cartridges had protected

the gunpowder. If his ammunition was ruined, he was
a goner.

The gunshots stopped. Belissari forced himself to
peer over the boulder, the cocked gun at his face. Not
that it would do any good against the sharpshooter.
Pecos—or whoever it was—was well out of pistol
range.

He took a deep breath and inched higher. Poseidon
stood patiently. *At least the assassin hasn't killed my
horse,* Belissari thought. Nothing. He was almost
standing now. *Maybe the guy was gone.*

Belissari never heard the next shot.

The bullet sliced a new part in his dark hair and
carved a furrow atop his head, dropping the horseman
behind the boulder in agony as he rocked on his
knees, dropping the gun and clutching his head with
both hands.

Tears flowed from the pain and Belissari drew up
in a ball, groaning, then forced himself into a sitting
position with his head bent low. He fought off unconsciousness but couldn't stop the nausea. He finally
toppled forward, face in the water, almost ready to
quit. Strength and determination returned almost immediately and he rose and leaned against the rock for
protection. His right hand crept out slowly and found
the single-action Colt, pulling it toward his body.

Biting back the pain, he wiped blood from his face
and ripped off his left shirtsleeve. He soaked it in the
pool of water and managed to clean the burning
wound, rinsing out the blood and repeating the pro-
cess a dozen times. Finally he placed the sleeve over
the bloody crease and forced his hat over it.

He tried to stand but couldn't, sinking and fighting

off another wave of nausea. His vision blurred but when he regained his focus, he stood again, teetering but not falling. "Let's finish this dance," he said aloud, turned, and ran toward Poseidon, whistling once and firing the Colt.

Chapter Ten

Poseidon answered Belissari's whistle by galloping toward him as the mustanger ran, firing the Colt above his head blindly. Belissari grabbed the reins as the horse reared and pulled himself beside the animal. The horse came down and nervously pranced as Belissari tried to find the stirrup. So far, the marksman in the rocks had not fired. Belissari lost his footing and stumbled onto the damp sand, but he maintained his viselike grip on the leather reins and revolver. Burning pain shot through his skull, and he grimaced and stumbled to his feet.

It took a Herculean effort, but on the second try he pulled himself clumsily into the saddle and kicked Poseidon hard. The horse turned and raced down the banks as Belissari fired once more, then leaned for-

78

ward and hugged the animal's neck, making himself a small target for the shooter.

But no one fired.

He kept Poseidon at a gallop until the stallion started to falter. Belissari reined in the animal behind a blood red lava boulder and reloaded his Colt. After a few minutes, he eased his grip on the reins and let Poseidon drink from the creek. He could use some water himself but he dared not dismount because he didn't think he could climb back in the saddle. He uncapped the canteen and took a few small sips, unsure if his stomach could keep even water down.

For some reason, the gunman in the rocks has stopped shooting. Belissari couldn't shake the thought. Four empty brass casings sparkled beside Poseidon's hooves, but Belissari knew that the chance of his hitting a man high in the rocks with a short-barreled .45 was remote.

"Yet he stopped shooting," Belissari told Poseidon, more to hear his own voice, to keep talking to fend off unconsciousness. "If he thought he killed me, he might have left." He shook his head. "But he would have come down to make sure I was finished. If he was leaving, he would have heard my shots and known I was still alive. He could have killed you, old boy," and he patted Poseidon's neck.

He looked back at the high canyon walls. A scrub jay sang in the trees and a rock squirrel ran down the creek's bank. *"Could I have hit him?"* he asked himself incredulously.

Shaking his head, he nudged Poseidon's ribs and the horse forded the creek, shallow here with a hard bed. Belissari looked over his shoulder, peering into

the dark rocks for a puff of smoke or the sun reflect-
ing off a rifle barrel. But he crossed the creek without
incident. He hugged the rocks closely as he continued
up the canyon and finally convinced himself that he
must have killed the assassin with a one-in-a-million
shot.

A bruise was forming on his left temple, blood was
crusted on his cheek and his hair was matted. Yet
most of the pain and all of the nausea had subsided
by the time Belissari cleared the canyon. Curving east,
he kept close to the rocks around a flat mesa and
followed along the base and dipped south for a mile
or so before turning into open country toward Horse
Thief Canyon.

Belissari crouched behind a scrubby juniper on the
top of the ridge, peering down at Roland Kibbee's
weathered shack. It was just a run-down adobe hut,
even worse than the last time Belissari had been here,
but Roland Kibbee was a disgusting man. Folks sometimes called him ''Maggot,'' even to his face.

Smoke climbed from the chimney and two bay
geldings were tethered to the hitching post in front of
the shack. The roof of the hut was thatched with
grass, wood, and debris; newspapers and calico
plugged holes in the crumbling stone. In the corral
were Hannah's horses and his own mustangs.

Belissari surmised that Kibbee's two visitors were
Rafe Malady's men but he guessed they wouldn't be
expecting him, figuring the gunman in the canyon had
done his job. Even so, he would play it carefully and
ease his way through the small trees and dark lava
rocks that covered the hillside like a checkerboard.

He thought about leaving Poseidon up here but decided that he probably would have to leave the trading post in a hurry. So he gathered the reins and began his careful descent, inching his way down the rugged hillside.

The horses in front of the shack were branded Bar R M—Malady's brand. Belissari tied Poseidon's reins to a branch of a little walnut tree on the north side of the hut, then quietly walked around the shack. One of the bays snorted but no sound came from inside the building.

He had to pick his way around the broken whiskey bottles, rusted cans, and rotting wagon spokes toward the corral. The trading post was squalid but Kibbee's corral was sturdy. The horses were content, grazing and resting after their hard run from Hannah's ranch. Three of Kibbee's mules were also in the corral, and a buckboard was parked underneath a lean-to. Belissari studied the terrain. A well stood a few yards from the gate, the only cover the yard offered. Horse Thief Canyon stretched northeast to southwest and offered little shelter for five or six hundred yards from Kibbee's. The shack had a side door, which he was facing, and the main entrance near the staked Malady horses.

He tugged on his Colt in the holster and moved quietly toward the side door. A lantern hung from the roof; rags and trash littered the ground below. He turned up the lantern and stared at the dirty side door. A crudely painted sign was nailed in place:

USE FRONT ENTRANCE

Belissari kicked the door off its hinges and stormed inside with his Colt drawn and cocked.

"What the—" red-haired Roland Kibbee began, but his words were lost as Belissari shot a hole in the makeshift roof, which sent dust flying and a rat screeching across the sod floor. In an instant he had the gun trained on the two cowboys sitting at a rough-hewn table in front of Kibbee's bar.

"Hello, Maggot," Belissari said, keeping the gun level.

"Belissari!" Kibbee shouted. "You ain't got no call to—"

"Don't I?"

Kibbee stood behind the bar, his hands held above his head. The bar was simply a one-by-eight-inch board nailed to two empty pickle barrels, topped with dirty glasses and foul-smelling whiskey. Rumor had it that Kibbee once was a Comanchero, selling liquor, guns—anything—to the Comanches, Kiowas, and Apaches until the Plains Indians surrendered. He might still deal with an occasional Mescalero, but mostly he traded in stolen horseflesh. Why no one had hanged him by now, Belissari didn't know. The horseman was well aware that his stench was awful, and with one sleeve missing and his head pasted with dried blood, he must look a sight. But compared to Kibbee, Belissari seemed fresh.

An uneven beard covered Kibbee's face, and the trader wore wire glasses with one lens missing. His boots were black calf sable-tips so old and rough and full of holes that they barely covered his threadbare socks, and he wore patched Levi's with frayed ends, grimy canvas suspenders, and a faded, stained undershirt with no buttons, revealing his white, hairless chest. A tattered gray-and-white polka-dot bandanna hung loosely around his neck, and his thick hair was partially covered by a gray herringbone Irish cap.

Kibbee wasn't carrying a gun, and from his panicked expression, Belissari dismissed him as a threat. He could also rule out at least one of the cowboys.

The youth sat to the left, his face drained of blood, clamping a stained rag against his left shoulder. He was pouring sweat, grasping a dirty jar in his left hand that held a liquid that probably would make pure mescal taste like fresh water. His hat lay upside down on the floor. Blood soaked his shirt front. This, Belissari guessed, was the rider he had shot at Hannah's ranch. He carried a Remington revolver in his gun belt but Belissari doubted that the kid had the nerve to pull his right hand from the bloody shoulder.

The older cowhand's eyes blazed beneath a pockmarked forehead. With the same blue eyes, turned-up nose, and cleft in the chin, he looked to be the wounded boy's brother, perhaps three or four years older. A linen duster was pushed around his gun holster but the man kept his hands flat on the table, far from the Colt.

"Still dealing with horse thieves, Maggot," Belissari stated.

The trader found his courage. "What are you talkin' about, Belissari? Them's Lyle and Bret Jackson and they ain't no horse thieves. Besides, them mustangs they brought in here ain't even wearin' a brand. You ain't got no call to—"

"Shut up!" Belissari bellowed. "I wouldn't let a band of Mescaleros take those horses from me and

I'm sure not going to give 'em up to you. Now I've been threatened, shot at, and haven't slept since I don't know when, and I'm in pretty foul humor. I'm takin' these horses back, and if anyone tries to stop me, I'll kill him.''

He moved to the front door and opened it, then walked toward the wounded boy, took his Remington, and tossed it outside. Next he grabbed the other cowhand's pistol and flung it out the door.

''Where's Buddy Pecos?'' the older cowboy asked.

''Dead,'' Belissari snapped. ''I killed him.'' That seemed to get everyone's attention. He slammed the front door and backed out of the shack, keeping his six-gun trained on the table. ''Like I said, anyone sticks his nose out of this establishment before I'm gone and I'll blow it off.'' He propped the busted side door in place, holstered his gun, and ran to Poseidon.

Belissari led the horse to the corral and was about to open the gate when the side door fell open and Kibbee stepped out with a shotgun, followed by both cowboys. They had regained their courage and called his bluff. And he hadn't bothered to check them for hideaway guns.

A pistol shot echoed and Belissari dived toward the well, pulling his gun as a second shot whipped over his head. Kibbee's shotgun discharged and sent the well bucket off its pulley.

His scalp wound reopened but he ignored it and flattened his back on the ground with his moccasins pressed against the well. Raising the Colt with both hands, he quickly aimed at the lantern below the roof. The .45 spoke and the kerosene lamp exploded, setting the roof and trash on fire. Belissari rocked to his knees and squeezed against the limestone well as another bullet ricocheted inches from his head.

The fire crackled, spreading instantly, and Kibbee screamed. Belissari heard the older Jackson shout, "Maggot, what are you doin'?"

That was all he needed. Belissari shot up and saw Kibbee slapping the fire with his hands, then dropping to his knees and flinging dirt at the spreading blaze. "My house!" he shouted. "My house!" Jackson turned away too late and saw Belissari. The cowboy swore loudly and was thumbing back the hammer when Belissari's Colt cracked. The man spun around, clutching his left side with both hands and sending his pistol to the ground as he dropped to his knees.

Kibbee picked up an old saddle blanket hanging on the corral fence and began beating out the remaining flames before the blaze could do too much damage to his home. The younger cowboy was leaning against the building, a heavy Colt hanging at his side, barrel pointed down. He was too weak to even lift the gun, and as Belissari stepped forward the kid slid down the wall and passed out.

Chapter Eleven

Once the flames and smoke had died, Belissari shoved the older Jackson inside and made Kibbee drag the unconscious brother into the hovel. He smashed Kibbee's shotgun against the corral and barked, "This time you stay inside or I kill everyone." He might have been angry enough to do it too. Belissari gathered the other weapons on the ground and dropped them in the well, then walked to the horses tied to the hitching rail. He pulled a battered Henry rifle from one scabbard and saw that the other saddle sheath was empty. Belissari recalled the gunfight at Hannah's ranch and remembered the wounded rider dropping the rifle. Belissari had left the weapon in the middle of the road.

Next he emptied the saddlebags' contents onto the ground. There were shaving kits, a pocket knife, spare socks, and longjohns. Satisfied that there were no more weapons, he returned to the well and dropped Jackson's repeater with an agreeable splash. He walked into the trading post with his Colt drawn. It was an unnecessary precaution, for Kibbee and Malady's men no longer posed a threat.

Bret Jackson, the older of the brothers, had unbuttoned his shirt and with both hands was stanching the flow of blood from the bullet hole in his side. His face was contorted with pain. Belissari glanced at the ashen Kibbee, who stood like a statue with both hands flat against the makeshift bar. Then he turned his attention to Bret Jackson.

The .45 slug had torn its way just above the man's waist, traveling a straight path and exiting in his back. The wound would cause much discomfort and loss of blood but it didn't appear serious.

He picked up one of Kibbee's whiskey jars and poured the alcohol over the cowboy's wounds. Bret Jackson yelped like a puppy and swayed in his chair. Belissari grinned with pleasure. He motioned at Jackson's bandanna with his pistol barrel. "Stick that in the holes, boy," he ordered. "It's a clean wound, and you won't die."

He couldn't say the same about Lyle Jackson, though.

Belissari moved toward the lad, now barely conscious on the cot in a corner. He knelt beside the younger Jackson and holstered his Colt. A board creaked behind him and Belissari barked without turning, "Hands on the bar, Maggot! Move and I'll kill you." Kibbee answered with a high-pitched apology.

Belissari peeled away the rag and shirt to examine the wound in the cowboy's shoulder.

A small bullet mold shaped like a pair of pliers lay on the floor by the cot and Belissari picked it up. This he used to pull out strands of thread and bits of cloth embedded in the bullet hole. He poured more whiskey to cleanse the injury and Jackson shrieked but surprisingly did not pass out. Belissari lifted the cowboy and glanced at his back but saw no exit wound.

He lowered the youth onto the cot. Their eyes met and Belissari spoke, surprised at the gentleness in his voice. These men had tried to kill him only minutes earlier. Some Texans would have shot or hanged them on the spot. But Pete Belissari was a mustanger and horse trader . . . not a man-killer.

"The bullet's still in there," he said. "If it doesn't come out soon, you'll die. You understand me?"

The cowboy nodded.

"I can't dig it out. I'm no doctor. Besides, I don't have the time and I owe you nothing. You think you can travel as far as Fort Stockton?"

Again the cowboy's head bobbed weakly.

"Maggot?" Belissari called.

"Yes sir, Mister Belissari," the trader responded. The horseman shook his head at Kibbee's blatant use of the courtesy title. *This coward once traded with the Comanches?*

He turned and faced Kibbee. "Maggot, I want you to hitch up your buckboard and take these two cowboys to the doctor in Fort Stockton."

"Why not Fort Davis?" Kibbee asked. "It's closer."

Belissari slowly rose. "I don't think that Rafe

Malady would be pleased to see these two in Fort Davis after he finds out that I've got my horses back.'' Bret Jackson glanced nervously at Belissari, and the horsemen knew his comment was more than a veiled threat.

"After you get patched up," Belissari told Bret Jackson, "light a shuck out of Texas. Because if I ever see you and your brother again I'll be inclined to press charges of horse theft—and you know what that will get you."

He scratched his neck for emphasis and walked outside.

After finding a long rawhide reata hanging on a corral post, Belissari gathered his mustangs and Hannah's two draft horses, looping the rope over their necks so that he could pull them rather than loose-herd the animals all the way to Fort Davis.

Roland Kibbee was busily hitching his mules to the buckboard when Belissari mounted Poseidon, opened the corral, and loped southwest toward Fort Davis, the horses behind him clouding the sky with thick dust.

Belissari slowed his pace after a mile. Soon afterward he stopped and studied Horse Thief Canyon. Satisfied that Kibbee and the Jackson brothers weren't trailing him—that would have surprised him, but it paid to be careful—Belissari eased Poseidon into a walk. His head throbbed again but he ignored it, and his eyes burned from dust and a lack of sleep.

There was an opening in the canyon to his left, a deer trail that meandered high into the rocks, and as he neared it he heard a horse whinny in the distance. He jerked Poseidon to a stop, listened intently. Wind ruffled oak leaves and a hawk screeched, but he also made out the faint sounds of iron horseshoes against hard rock. *Buddy Pecos?* Belissari thought. He dropped from the saddle and pulled the horses to the side of the canyon, covering Poseidon's nose with his left hand and drawing the Colt. But he couldn't stop all of the horses from answering the rider's horse, and if Pecos heard one—if it was Pecos—he'd be in trouble. His one chance was to surprise the gunman as he rounded the entrance into Horse Thief Canyon.

Sweat dampened his forehead and stung his eyes as Belissari gritted his teeth, waiting for what seemed an eternity. Finally the horseman caught sight of the roan gelding and its tall, one-eyed rider as they appeared out of the rocks.

Buddy Pecos sprayed tobacco juice against a rock as Belissari called out: "Hands up!"

Rafe Malady's foreman peered at Belissari with an amused expression in his good eye. He shifted the wad of tobacco in his mouth and slowly raised his hands. Only then did Belissari finally exhale.

"You're one tough hombre," Pecos said finally.

Belissari ignored him. "With your left hand," he directed, "I want you to pull out your six-gun and throw it into the rocks."

Pecos nodded but first wrapped his reins around the saddle horn. He kept his right hand high in the air, then pulled a heavy Schofield .45 from the holster. Though he hadn't been told to do so, he opened the top-break revolver and dropped six bullets onto the ground, snapped the gun shut, and tossed it against the canyon rocks.

He was cautiously reaching for the Sharps rifle in

the scabbard with his left hand when Belissari checked him. It wasn't a threatening move. Pecos simply planned on throwing the rifle into the rocks as he had done the Smith and Wesson. But Belissari wasn't about to leave this man with a long gun. Not the way he could shoot.

"The 'Big Fifty' stays where it is," he said. Pecos stopped. "Just swing off your horse and tie him to the end of my string." Pecos did as he was told as Belissari kept his gun trained on him. Sluggishly the man walked back until he faced the mustanger, leaned his towering frame against a rock, reached into his vest pockets, and withdrew the makings of a cigarette. He spit out the plug of tobacco and stared at the horseman.

Belissari didn't know what to make of the gunman's demeanor. But he was riled. "I reckon I had you pegged wrong," he said as he swung into the saddle. The Colt never wavered from Pecos. "I didn't think you were the kind of man who'd bushwhack someone in a canyon with a long gun. And I sure didn't think you'd shoot at a house full of orphans and a young woman in the middle of the night."

"The kids and gal all right?" Pecos asked.

"Scared out of a year's growth, thanks to you. But they could have been killed." Belissari shook his head at the gunman's audacity. Here was a man who raided an orphanage under the cover of darkness, then had the gall to ask about the children's well-being the next morning.

"Give me one good reason why I shouldn't shoot you down," Belissari snapped.

The gunman stuck the cigarette in the corner of his

mouth and shrugged. "Can't very well stop you, can I?" he said, returned the tobacco pouch and paper in his vest, and withdrew a match.

Belissari controlled his temper. "I'm riding out, Pecos. I'll stake your horse a mile or two up the canyon. You can pick it up there. And I'll give you the same advice I gave your saddle pals back at Maggot's: Ride out of Texas."

"Sounds like good advice." Casually Pecos struck the match against his belt buckle, cupped his hands, and lit the cigarette. He took a deep drag and exhaled with pleasure, the smoke curling upward past his scarred face.

Belissari kicked Poseidon into a trot, peering over his shoulder every few seconds. A hundred yards up the canyon he stopped and turned around for a better view. Buddy Pecos still leaned against the boulder, calmly smoking the cigarette. The gunman looked up and gave Belissari a friendly salute.

"That's the strangest son of a gun I've ever met," Belissari told Poseidon as he kicked the horse toward Fort Davis.

Chapter Twelve

He left Horse Thief Canyon and turned westward, crossed Limpia Creek again, and picked up the main road, climbing Wild Rose Pass, passing the still-smoldering barn, and not stopping until he crested the hill overlooking Fort Davis. After the horses caught their wind, he eased his way toward the sprawling military base and dusty adobe town about a mile down the old Overland Trail.

The fort stood at the foot of Limpia Canyon, its palisaded hills towering above the stone, adobe, and picket structures. Several soldiers, black cavalry troopers and white infantrymen, stared at him as he trotted past the quartermaster's store and forage house on his left.

Belissari could understand those stares. After all, here was a man pulling a string of horses. A man with

93

a battered face, clothes caked with mud, one shirt-sleeve missing, and a hat that looked as if it had been trampled by stampeding buffalo.

Past those quartermaster buildings lay a massive adobe corral, which was a flurry of activity as black-smiths hammered and mules brayed. And just beyond that were the bustling cavalry corrals where Belissari reined up as a tall black farrier in dirty white trousers and stable frock met him with a smile.

"Hello, Mister Petros," the man greeted.

"Josiah." Belissari handed the reata to the soldier. "The two draft horses aren't mine, but if you'd let Captain Kaye know that the others are his if his price is right, I'd appreciate it."

The soldier nodded and led the horses into the cor-rals.

"Sir!" a voice boomed to his right, and Belissari turned to see a lean black man briskly approaching. He wore a tan campaign hat, navy blouse, and blue trousers. Brass buttons and brilliant patent leather glistened. On his sleeves shone the yellow chevrons of a sergeant major. He was spit-and-polish Army all the way.

The noncommissioned officer snapped to attention in front of him and looked him over with disgust. "The sight of you, sir—indeed the smell of you, sir—is turning my men's stomachs. I would be obliged if you would depart Fort Davis for town."

"Hello, Sergeant Major Cadwallader," Belissari said drily.

"Mister Belissari," Cadwallader said, unsmiling, "you have outdone yourself this time."

Belissari could only nod. "Cad," he said, "you

reckon I could borrow a horse to ride to town?'' He patted Poseidon's soaking neck. "My gray is all done in.''

"This is not a civilian livery, Mister Belissari,'' the sergeant major replied. "I suggest you try in town.'' When the horseman frowned, the soldier stepped back, at ease, and reconsidered. "However, in view of your dealings with this man's army, I suppose we could make some arrangement.''

He snapped ramrod straight and barked, "Trooper Washington!'' Josiah rounded the corner in double time, fell into attention, and jerked a salute. "Trooper, saddle Mister Belissari''—Cadwallader's eyes twinkled with amusement—"a mule.''

Belissari didn't bother to argue. He wearily dismounted and let Josiah take Poseidon to the corrals. In a few minutes, he returned with a saddled, floppy-eared mule and helped the exhausted horseman mount. Cadwallader stood at ease, unsmiling, but Belissari knew the soldier was enjoying himself immensely.

"Cad, has a young woman been here this morning to see Doctor Leslie? Maybe with some children?''

"She was here late this morning. The captain patched her up and she went in to town.''

"How is she?''

"Captain Leslie said she'll be fine.''

Belissari breathed easier. He tried to remember the name of the minister. *Cox.* He asked Cadwallader if he knew the reverend.

This time Cadwallader smiled. "Soldiers and preachers don't go hand in hand, Mister Belissari,'' the sergeant major said, "but if I were you, I might try the Presbyterian church in town.'' He turned and walked away, calling out, ''Have that mule back here by water call, sir.''

When Belissari turned around he saw Trooper Josiah Washington grinning broadly. ''That church is on the edge of town, Mister Petros. On the right. If you gets to the stage stop and wagon yard, you's gone too far.''

Belissari thanked the soldier and was about to ride off when Washington stopped him. ''Mister Petros?''

''Yeah?''

''If I was you, I'd go pay me two bits for a bath and puts on some new clothes before I went visiting some female.''

The horseman grinned. ''I look that bad, huh, Josiah?''

''That ain't the half of it, Mister Petros. I'm standing downwind of you.''

The town of Fort Davis was typically a dusty adobe village in the Davis Mountains that got a little rowdy when the soldiers got paid or some cowboys came to town, but for the most part it was quiet and subdued. Belissari, however, was surprised as he rode the mule toward town. Horses crowded every hitching rail. Red, white, and blue banners streamed over the streets, flapping in the breeze. And men, women, and children lined the plank boardwalks. His mouth watered and stomach knotted as he smelled tobacco, coffee, beans, and frying meat.

He couldn't understand the excitement, the crowd, until he saw the placard nailed to a wood column in front of the Fort Davis Bank. How could he have forgotten about that horse race?

A church steeple rose above the adobe buildings and occasional juniper, and he steered the mule in its direction. Hannah ran from the church as soon as he rounded the corner. Her right hand was covered with white bandages, arm held in a sling. Forgetting his own weariness, he leaped off the mule and they embraced for a few seconds, pulling away when the children and a white-haired minister rushed from the church.

"You look horrible," Hannah told him.

They sat on a swing hanging from an oak limb behind the church, enjoying the quiet. Belissari finished telling her about the shootout at Kibbee's and Buddy Pecos, and she related her walk to town earlier that morning.

"All I could think of," she said after a few minutes of silence, "was you. The ranch really doesn't matter. I can start over somewhere. Maybe. But if you had gotten killed . . ."

He put his arm around her shoulder and pulled her close. "I have to see Captain Kaye about those mustangs," he said. He swallowed. "Hannah, we can't get a thousand dollars by Monday. I think we can take your case to the courts. Maybe win. But it will take time."

She pulled away from him. "You're saying I've lost the ranch." There was an edge to her voice. This was the angry woman who was ready to thrash him when he had ridden into her life Friday morning.

"You said you didn't care about it a minute ago."

"That was different."

He sighed in defeat. "Times change, Hannah. I'm not giving up . . . yet. But I think you—and those kids—need to be prepared for what might happen Monday morning."

Hannah sprung away, her face reddening in anger. She stuttered for a moment and finally exhaled. She breathed deeply, calming herself. "You're right. But I'm still not ready to surrender. Not to a man like Rafe Malady."

"Neither am I," Belissari said. His knees popped as he rose. "We both need to clear our minds. Relax. How about dinner tonight?"

Hannah nodded.

"Seven o'clock. Lempert Hotel. I'll meet you there."

He climbed aboard the mule.

"Pete?"

"Yes ma'am?"

"Bathe first."

Sergeant Major Robert Cadwallader met Belissari at the cavalry corrals and escorted him past the barracks and across the parade ground. The American flag snapped in the wind as they briskly continued toward Officer's Row, the procession of adobe and stone houses that lined the other end of the parade ground. They cut between two houses and continued toward the post commander's stable.

"Cad," Belissari finally called out, "where are you taking me?"

"When I explained your condition to Captain Kaye, he ordered me to take you to the post hospital for a bath and to have Captain Leslie check you over.''

The stone hospital stood on the far west end of the fort. The two men climbed the stairs and Cadwallader opened the door. Belissari entered slowly, the smell of alcohol dominating the inside of the building. Cadwallader's boots thumped across the hardwood floor as he opened a white door and motioned Belissari inside.

Belissari hated doctors and especially hospitals. He nervously went into the room and saw a washtub on the floor, water steaming. On a wooden chair beside the tub was a towel, bar of soap, cigar, and newspaper. A pair of store-bought blue and red striped pants and a crimson collarless shirt, both neatly folded, lay on the narrow cot in the far corner.

This might not be so bad after all, Belissari thought as he began undressing. Cadwallader slammed the door shut.

Soaking in the tub, cigar in his mouth, Belissari had almost forgotten how good a bath could feel and he hadn't tasted a good cigar in almost a year. Trumpet calls sounded faintly outside but Belissari ignored them. This felt like heaven. He unfolded the four-page newspaper and studied it. *The Presidio County News.* Fort Davis, Texas, Saturday, May 31, 1884. It was even today's paper. Now that was service. *Yes sir, this is heaven.*

He started with the heading ''News Items'' in the left-hand corner of the first page and began reading. He was up to the third column and the heading ''Political News and Views'' when the door opened and Doctor Jack Leslie entered.

Captain Leslie was a robust man with black hair and a handlebar mustache. He was sixty-two years old but looked fifty with his ruddy complexion and green eyes. He wore Army-issue trousers and boots and a white surgeon's frock over his gray wool shirt. In his left hand he carried a shiny handsaw. That got Belissari's attention. But the doctor tossed the instrument onto a table, ignoring Belissari, and began to root through several bottles.

He found what he needed and carried it past Belissari to the other end of the room as if the horseman were invisible. Belissari heard the doctor opening some more jars and mumbling to himself. The horseman sighed, put aside the paper, leaned back, and closed his eyes. The lukewarm water was lulling him to sleep.

Jack Leslie pulled up behind Belissari and gently fingered the crease in the horseman's scalp. "Does this hurt?" he asked softly.

"No," Belissari said sleepily.

"How about this?"

The cigar fell out of Belissari's mouth as the horseman screamed. His head felt as if it were on fire and he slipped in the tub and went under, coming up coughing and spitting out soapy water as Captain Leslie cackled like a hen. Belissari was on his knees. He balled his fists and rubbed his eyes as the stinging in his head ceased. Blood throbbed in his temples. He coughed again. Jack Leslie stopped laughing, caught his wind, and erupted once more.

"Doc," Belissari finally bellowed, "you've got the bedside manners of a scorpion!"

Leslie's laughter slowly died. "Pete, that's what you get for smoking in my hospital," he said and walked toward his surgeon's kit. "Now dry yourself off, put on your pants, and let me look at those cuts."

Chapter Thirteen

Jack Leslie's fingers were gentle now, deftly applying medicine to Belissari's head wound. The horseman sat in a chair facing the white door as the Army doctor clipped the hair around the crease and softly dabbed it with a damp cloth.

"You're a lucky man, Pete," Leslie stated matter-of-factly. "Couple of inches lower and you'd be a client for the undertaker."

Belissari grunted. "An inch higher and he would have missed," he said.

Leslie laughed good-naturedly—not his henlike cackle earlier. He clipped some more, sat aside his scissors, and applied a bandage across Belissari's scalp. "Doesn't need any stitches, though it'll probably leave a scar and definitely will be sore for a few days. But you've got a nice head of hair, young man, and I think it'll grow over your new part.''

Belissari looked up and stared at a mirror on the wall. A narrow strip of white cloth interrupted the dark hair on top of his head. ''I wouldn't worry about manners so much,'' the doctor said. ''Just keep your hat on until most of this hair grows back.''

Leslie applied some salve to the cut and bruise above Belissari's temple and scrubbed the glass cuts on his hand. He stepped aside, looked the horseman over for a few seconds, and nodded. ''You'll live.''

''How much do I owe you?''

''Two dollars.''

''I can't pay you until Vernon pays me.''

Leslie only shrugged.

''I'd like to pay for Hannah Scott too.''

This time Leslie shook his head. ''No charge for treating her, son.'' Leslie studied Belissari again, leaned forward, and tapped the dark temple with more medicine.

''You have a mighty fine friend in that young lady, Pete,'' the doctor said. ''She came storming in here this morning, screaming for help. Not for her, mind you. She wanted to get a troop of cavalry out after you. She even barged into Colonel Grierson's office and demanded action.''

''What did Ben say?''

''The colonel explained that he had no jurisdiction in civilian cases. But he promised that he would write the attorney general and the United States marshal, and he sent his adjutant to town to make sure the county sheriff at least sent a posse after you.''

Belissari smiled.

"The sheriff rode out but I doubt if he got past Hannah's ranch. He has Rafe Malady's brand all over his sorry hide. If you hadn't shown up by stable call, though, I think Captain Kaye and Sergeant Major Cadwallader would have led some troopers over the wall to find you."

"Cadwallader? I always figured that he hated my guts."

The doctor laughed. "It's the sergeant major's duty to make everyone on this post—civilian and military—think he detests them. He couldn't do his job if they felt otherwise. No, Pete, you have a lot of friends in this man's army. . . . Of course, I'm not one of them."

Leslie stepped back and motioned toward the crimson shirt. Belissari enjoyed the man's banter. The horseman stood and carefully pulled the cotton garment over his head and stuck the tails in his new pants. His moccasins and hat were the same, but Belissari felt like a new man. Captain Leslie was cleaning his instruments in a tin basin of alcohol.

"Doc," Belissari said, "you wouldn't have three hundred and twenty-five dollars you could loan me, would you?"

Leslie cackled again. "Son," he said after gathering his wits, "the paymaster's slow this month and most of my civilian customers, like you, are tight with a dollar coin. I'd like to help you and Miss Scott but . . ." He shrugged.

"I know. I just find it hard to believe the town would let Malady get away with all he's done."

"The town isn't so bad, Pete. It's just that the Malady brothers bring a lot of business to this part of

West Texas. Now if you could prove that Malady
burned down that barn, why, those Texicans would
run that ruffian out on a rail.''

''It was his men.''

''His lawyer brother would just argue that Rafe
didn't know what they were doing, and Malady's men
would be too scared to say otherwise.

''Let me tell you about Rafe Malady. About a year
ago he was playing poker in a saloon on the south
side of town. He got taken pretty good, for a few
dollars, I hear. That night, he rode back into town and
burned that saloon to the ground. No one was inside.''

''Why wasn't he arrested for that?''

''Because he owned the saloon.'' Leslie tapped his
left temple. ''The man's a bit . . . peculiar. But one of
these days he'll get his comeuppance and land in jail,
on the gallows, or in the crazy ward.''

The door shot open and Sergeant Major Cadwallader entered, clicking his heels like a pistol shot and
sharply saluting Leslie. ''Sir! Sergeant Major
Cadwallader reporting to escort Mister Belissari to
Captain Kaye's office to negotiate the sale of mustangs. Sir!''

Annoyed, Leslie waved off the salute. ''Take him,
Sergeant Major.''

Vernon Kaye was a lanky man in his early fifties,
with flowing Dundreary whiskers and a bushy gray
mustache. Belissari had always guessed that the captain grew the long sideburns to make up for the bald
top of his head. He was an officer of the Tenth Cavalry and was responsible for the purchase of horses
for the regiment of buffalo soldiers at Fort Davis.

Kaye was also a man who didn't always believe in the Army manual when it came to horseflesh.

Kaye stared out of his office window at the corrals, absentmindedly combing his whiskers with his fingers as Belissari sat on a hard bench and waited. Finally Kaye asked, "Whose brand are they wearing?"

And Belissari held back a grin as he responded to the old joke. "Well, mostly I'm wearing theirs." Of course, most of the injuries he sported today were from Rafe Malady's men, not those nine mustang mares.

"I'd say that by tomorrow they'll be wearing a U.S. brand. How 'bout a shot of ouzo to celebrate?"

Kaye walked to his desk, opened a drawer, and poured a shot of clear liquid, which he handed to the startled mustanger. Belissari smelled the liqueur, then tasted it. It *was* ouzo. Real Greek ouzo. Kaye smiled. "I figured you might get a kick out of that."

Belissari leaned back on the bench. He downed the rest of the alcohol and placed the empty glass on Vernon's desk. Kaye dropped his lean frame into the leather chair and dabbed a pen in an inkwell.

"You entering tomorrow's race?" Kaye asked casually.

"No. I've seen that thoroughbred the Comanches are entering."

"So have we. But Sergeant Major Cadwallader will be riding that dun you sold us last year."

Belissari shook his head. "No offense, Vernon, but I've never sold you any horse that could outrace that thoroughbred. What's that the Comanches call him? Lightning Flash."

"Perhaps," Kaye replied easily. "But this is no

romp around a horse oval. It's an all-out dash down Main Street, past the fort, across Limpia Creek down the valley, and back. It'll be war. And Sergeant Major Cadwallader is a fine horseman.''

''No offense again, Vernon, but I've never seen anyone who could fork a horse like a Comanche.''

Kaye nodded. ''The Comanche horse is the betting favorite. Though people say Rafe Malady is entering a sleek racer.''

''Malady. That fat old man's going to race?''

''He's a good horseman despite his size.''

Belissari shook his head and Kaye changed the subject. ''I'll make out a voucher for six hundred and seventy-five dollars. You can wire it to San Antonio or cash it in at your bank in Corpus Christi—''

''Vernon.''

Kaye looked up.

''Any chance I could get cash?''

The captain set aside his pen and frowned. Belissari continued: ''Hannah Scott needs one thousand dollars by Monday or she'll lose her ranch to Rafe Malady.''

Kaye's expression was blank.

Belissari stammered. He didn't know what else to say.

''Pete,'' his friend said after several seconds, ''I'd love to help. I don't want to see those orphans turned out on the streets any more than you. But the fact of the matter is I don't have that much cash money on hand. And secondly''—Kaye paused, then burst out— ''Pete, I'm getting married in September.''

Belissari was thunderstruck. A smile finally carved itself on his face and he stood up and offered Kaye his hand. They shook warmly. "That's great, Vernon. Who's the lucky lady?"

"Congressman Little's daughter. In San Antonio."

Belissari whistled. Kaye's bald head turned beet red, and he busied himself signing the voucher. He handed it to the horseman, who stuck it inside his shirt.

"Married?" Belissari whistled again. "To a congressman's daughter. Vernon, I never knew you had it in you."

The captain's head bobbed in embarrassment. "Hope you'll come to the wedding."

"Wouldn't miss it."

Belissari picked up his hat and turned to walk away. "Thanks for the ouzo, Vernon. And congratulations. Sorry about asking about the money. I didn't mean to put you on the spot."

"Pete."

Kaye pointed to the bench as Belissari turned around. The horseman swallowed and sank into the bench. Something was wrong.

"Pete," Kaye repeated. "I'll be resigning my commission after I get married. I'm going to . . . well, I'm going be selling tinware."

Belissari couldn't suppress a smile. "There will be a new officer here and I seriously doubt if he'll be willing to pay seventy-five dollars for mustangs," Kaye said. The ouzo turned in Belissari's stomach. The smile vanished.

The captain sighed. "Pete, I've been hard-pressed to explain why I pay that much for cavalry mounts when bigger horses can been bought a lot cheaper.

Headquarters hasn't been pleased with our spending habits at Fort Davis.''

"Yes, but you and I both know that those mustangs are what you need to track down Apaches. Not grain-fed Army mounts. You said it yourself. It takes an Apache to track an Apache, and an Apache mustang to chase down an Apache mustang.''

"The Apache wars are over, Pete. The Army isn't going to buy your mustangs anymore.''

Belissari sank back. He felt as if he had been kicked in the belly. Kaye moved toward his friend and sat beside him, putting his arm on the horseman's shoulder.

"You're a young man, Pete. You're great with horses. Ranches will still be interested in mustangs. And you could get yourself a spread, raise horses there. You'd be good at it. It's not like you have to go selling *tinware*.''

Both men forced smiles.

"You should get married, start a ranch, raise a brood of kids and horses. But you have to admit that mustanging isn't what it once was. Twenty, thirty years back, those wild horses were everywhere for the taking all across South and West Texas. You told me yourself that when you were just a boy one of your daddy's deck hands took you horse hunting just a day's ride from Corpus.''

"That's when I knew what I wanted to do.''

"Well, look at yourself today. You spent two months in those mountains and all you could bring in was nine mustangs. Ten years ago you could have found a hundred. You were just born too late, friend.''

"Yeah.''

"Times change, Pete. I just want you to be prepared for it."

Belissari nodded. "I was pretty much telling someone that earlier this afternoon." He slowly rose and headed for the door.

"Thanks, Vernon."

As he stepped outside, Kaye added softly, "Pete, even Odysseus had to put away his oars."

"I know." Belissari softly closed the door.

Chapter Fourteen

As he saddled Poseidon he realized he had made a mistake walking out of Kaye's office that way. The voucher was tucked inside his shirt, but he had no cash money on him. None. And although he probably could use the signed bill to get credit for a hotel room and to board Poseidon at a livery, he wasn't sure if a restaurant would accept it. Come to think of it, he wasn't sure if he could get credit from a hotel or livery either.

This was, after all, Rafe Malady's town.

That left him with three options. He could walk back to see Vernon Kaye and look like an idiot by asking for a loan or he could cancel his date with Hannah. He immediately ruled out those choices, particularly the latter, and turned to face his third alternative.

"Sergeant Major Cadwallader," Belissari asked the lean, black soldier, "you reckon you could spare a few bucks until the bank opens Monday?"

Cadwallader's face remained stony. "Mister Belissari," he barked, "I am a noncommissioned officer in the United States Tenth Cavalry, not a bank teller."

"Yes sir," Belissari said.

"Besides, the paymaster is late again this month."

"Yes sir."

"Why, pray tell, would an entrepreneur such as yourself need money?"

"Well, I could use a hotel room."

"All the hotels in town are full because of the race. The closest place you could find a bed is in Marfa, and I'm including all houses of ill repute."

"I'd stay in a livery or wagon yard with my horse."

"Every livery stable and wagon yard is also full— with livestock, poor folks, and cowboys. And one gentleman from Kentucky rented Jeff Coady's entire livery for his thoroughbred, which he's entering in the race."

"Well, I can sleep outside. That's no problem. But I'm supposed to be taking this young lady out to supper tonight, and—"

Cadwallader reached inside his blouse and withdrew a brown leather billfold. He placed two U.S. greenbacks in Belissari's hands. "I'm not so heartless that I would interrupt your romance, sir. But I expect interest on that ten dollars. A beer, a rye, and a cigar at Lightner's Saloon first thing Monday evening."

"You've got it."

"And when you're done with your romancing, sir,

I suppose we could let you sleep in our stables, considering your services with this man's army. See Trooper Washington upon your return.''

"Thank you, Sergeant Major," Belissari said with a wide grin as he swung into his saddle. The thanks were genuine. Ten dollars was a lot of money for a soldier to loan. Maybe Doctor Leslie had been right—the iron sergeant really did like him.

"A beer, a rye, and a cigar, mister!" Cadwallader called after Belissari as he loped toward town.

Every hitching rail was full in town, and Cadwallader had not been exaggerating about the livery stables. The town of Fort Davis was busting like a two-dollar mare gorged on oats. It seemed that everybody in West Texas, along with every gambler or horseman west of the Pecos River, had descended upon the Davis Mountains for the big race.

Belissari had to tether Poseidon in an alley as he went to Charles Buehler's bakery near the courthouse to buy some candy for the orphans. Whistling as he rounded the corner, carrying the brown sack of peppermint sticks in his left hand, he never saw the hard fist that slammed into his jaw and dropped him in an explosion of dust.

Belissari's vision was blurred as he struggled to rise, aware of the spilled candy in the dusty alley. Someone helped him to his feet, and when his vision cleared, Belissari recognized the ugly, malevolent face of Buddy Pecos.

Malady's gunman smiled as his right fist rocketed into Belissari's stomach. The horseman gasped for air, doubled over, and waited for another blow. It came as expected. The punch in the right temple knocked his vision out of sorts again and forced him back into the dust. His teeth snapped together as he landed on his butt with a hard thud.

Pecos slowly walked toward Belissari, bent over and jerked the dazed horseman to his feet. Belissari heard laughter and saw a handful of Malady's riders watching in amusement. Pecos's grin was out of place on his scarred face, Belissari thought, as the gunman brushed dirt off his clothes.

"Sorry, Mister Horseman," Pecos said, "but you've worn out your welcome."

The gunman drew back to deliver another savage punch, but Belissari had recovered his wits. A sudden wave of anger coursed through his veins, and he blocked Pecos's blow with his left arm while dispensing a roundhouse right that connected solidly against the gunman's jaw. The punch caught Pecos's unawares and sent him back a couple of steps, killing his men's laughter in an instant. Pecos's smile likewise disappeared, and his cruel eye darkened.

He took a step, balling his fists tighter, but Belissari was upon him quickly. The horseman's right staggered the gunman again, and he followed quickly with short, crisp, violent blows, driving Pecos toward the main street. Belissari felt his right fist connect against the gunman's oft-broken nose, which spurted blood.

Buddy Pecos's face was contorted in pain, red with anger, but he was used to fighting. Belissari followed a left undercut against the man's chin with a solid, crunching swing into the leathery cowboy's stomach. Pecos gasped for air, and Belissari took time to fill his own lungs.

Despite the furious blows, Pecos was still standing. Some time later, Belissari would come to respect the man's fighting ability, but for the moment, Belissari was thinking of nothing but pummeling the gunman into the Fort Davis dirt. He connected again, dodged a right easily, and felt some left knuckles skin his ear. Belissari faked twice with his left, then sent a right toward the man's bloody nose.

But Pecos deflected the shot, reached out, and grabbed Belissari's face. His thumb accidentally slipped into Belissari's mouth, so the horseman clamped down on it with his teeth. For the first time, Pecos vocalized an awareness of pain. He yelped and pulled his hand from Belissari.

Biting wasn't exactly fair fighting, but Belissari didn't consider this a fair fight.

Pecos shook his right hand and stuck his thumb in his mouth for a second, then charged Belissari furiously. The horseman simply ducked and the tall cowhand went sailing over him, almost disappearing in a cloud of dust. Pecos rolled underneath Poseidon, which snorted and panicked, trying to get away from the angry form underneath him.

When Pecos found his feet, Belissari charged and deftly slammed his right shoulder into the man's side. The two crashed against the gray horse, which whinnied and broke its tether, sending the two fighters to the ground as the horse darted out of the alley.

The two men leaned against each other, panting heavily. Belissari managed to push the taller man away, then drew back and drilled his right fist above the man's ear. Pecos toppled, and struggled to his feet, far from finished, but Belissari was up first and was moving in to end this fight now.

His punch missed. The momentum carried him forward and before he could recover, Pecos has wrapped his long, sinewy arms around him. The gunman squeezed, but Belissari shifted, broke his right arm free and rifled his elbow against his assailant's sternum. Pecos coughed, and Belissari pulled away, breaking the gunman's grip. Belissari turned on his heels and connected with a quick left that split Pecos's lower lip.

Again, Belissari pumped his lungs for fresh air. His head wounds throbbed beneath his hat, surprisingly still clamped on his head, and he felt and smelled fresh blood on his face. Sweat stung his eyes. He blinked, licked his lips, and moved forward.

This close to the courthouse, Belissari had hoped the fight would have attracted the law by now. But he seemed to recall that the sheriff was supposedly a Malady man. He heard commotion behind him and some of Pecos's cohorts saying, "Move along, folks, this is just a friendly fight. . . . Move along, folks. . . . Everything's all right."

Belissari was alone. Help would not come. It was just him against this "Cyclops," and then maybe Malady's other men.

Pecos was much taller than Belissari. He outweighed Belissari by thirty pounds, had more reach with his bony, tough fists, and was a veteran of alley brawls. Belissari knew this. He realized that his only chance at winning this fight was to finish it now. He wouldn't be able to outlast the gunman much longer.

He blocked Pecos's right with his arm and followed

with a left that Pecos easily deflected. Both men were tired. Pecos tried to blink sweat out of his eyes, and Belissari took advantage. He sent three furious jabs into the giant's temple that sent Pecos staggering. The gunman wavered but didn't fall.

Belissari tried to draw back his right arm for a knockout punch, but his body wouldn't respond.

Something suddenly jerked Belissari back and he felt a burning in his arms and chest. He looked down to see his arms pinned against his torso by a hemp rope as he was pulled violently away from Pecos. The cowhands had roped him.

Buddy Pecos, face bloodied, eyes puffy, was walking toward him. *He doesn't look happy,* Belissari thought.

"Mama Hannah!" Cynthia shouted. "You're all dressed up!"

Hannah stepped away from the mirror and brushed some stray hairs into place with her fingers. She wore a two-piece blue cotton dress trimmed with red velvet. The dress sported a stand-up collar, dove-tailed back, and a bright red bow around the waist. It was the nicest dress she owned. She hadn't worn it in three years.

She had bathed that afternoon, washed her hair, powdered herself with lilac. Her stomach fluttered from nerves about tonight. *It's only dinner,* she told herself. *I know nothing about Pete Belissari.* But she knew enough. She stepped back from the Chippendale mirror and forced a smile.

"I ain't never seen you so beautiful," a wide-eyed Cynthia said.

" 'I haven't ever,' " Hannah corrected. "Don't say 'ain't.' "

"Yes ma'am."

"Land's sakes, child," the Reverend Cox told her and kissed her cheek. "You're absolutely stunning."

Hannah couldn't help herself. "Am I?"

The white-haired preacher smiled and nodded. "I don't lie, Miss Scott. That young fellow is a mighty lucky man."

Hannah's butterflies disappeared as she walked out of the house toward the Lempert Hotel. "A mighty lucky man," Cox called after her.

Buddy Pecos wiped his bloody nose across a torn shirtsleeve. His chest heaved for a minute as he stared at the bound horseman in front of him. Finally, the gunman creaked, "Turn him loose."

"What?" one of the cowhands snapped in bewilderment.

"I said turn him loose!" Pecos exploded. "I ain't beatin' a man like him this way. I fights fair."

"No," a voice commanded.

Belissari and Pecos turned their heads. Leaning against the bakery was a middle-aged man with a red mustache and goatee and black broadcloth suit. Belissari's eyes fastened on the six-pointed brass star pinned on the man's lapel.

"No," the sheriff repeated in an Irish accent. "You've wasted enough time. Now finish it and get this gent out of town before someone recognizes him or one of his Army buddies shows up. Move!"

But Pecos refused to budge, and Belissari's respect for his enemy increased. Finally, another cowhand emerged in front of the bound horseman. He smiled as he drew back to punch. Belissari simply kicked the young cowboy in the knee. The cowhand cried out in amazement and pain and crashed to the dirt. For once, Belissari wished he wore boots; they would have done a lot more damage than his moccasins. And out of the corner of his eye, Belissari thought he saw Buddy Pecos smile.

The kicked cowboy wasn't grinning when he regained his feet, though. He limped over, ears burning with anger, and slammed a hard fist into Belissari's forehead. The horseman's head snapped back, and the cowhand followed with several blows to the head and stomach. In a minute, Belissari dropped to his knees. The rope binding his arms slackened, and the horseman toppled forward, still conscious, but out of it.

"Now tie him up and get rid of him," Belissari heard the sheriff say.

The speeding buckboard caught Hannah's attention as she walked to the hotel restaurant. The cowboy driving it was letting curses fly while whipping the two horses furiously as he sped out of town. He was followed by a half-dozen riders loping behind him toward the desert. Hannah's throat went dry when she recognized one of the riders. *Buddy Pecos.*

She watched with others as the riders disappeared in the dust. An elderly woman criticized the cowboys and the sheriff for letting folks drive that way. Someone could get hurt. Hannah agreed and walked to the restaurant.

Peering in the window, she saw that Belissari

wasn't there, so she stood outside on the boardwalk, enjoying the evening breeze. A gentleman in a brocade vest and derby hat rose from his seat on the bench in front of the hotel. He flicked away cigar ash and said in a rich Southern accent, "Ma'am, would you care for a seat?"

Hannah nodded politely and sat down as the man tipped his hat and disappeared into the crowd along the boardwalk. She crossed her legs and waited for Pete Belissari.

Chapter Fifteen

The buckboard lurched violently as it turned sharply along the makeshift road, sending Belissari rolling and crashing against the wagon's side. Something sharp bit into his shoulder. His arms were bound tightly behind his back and another rope secured his ankles. The wagon hit a hole and Belissari flew up and landed with a thud, sending pain the length of his body.

He had been covered with a scratchy woolen blanket, but between Belissari's movements and the buckboard driver's insanity the horseman now lay on top of the blanket. Someone hurled loud profanities—it sounded like Buddy Pecos—and the buckboard finally slowed to a reasonable gait. That was good, Belissari thought, because the horses couldn't endure this pain much longer, and neither could he.

Belissari forced himself into a halfway seated position, leaning awkwardly against the seat of the buckboard. He now recognized the driver as the youthful cowboy who had finished whipping him after Pecos refused to continue. The kid ignored him and concentrated on his task. Pecos rode ahead of them, and the other cowboys galloped behind.

To his right, Belissari saw the tall, rugged form of Mitre Peak. That surprised him, for it meant they were headed south. He had expected to be delivered to the Malady ranch north of town.

Hours later they passed a small village along the railroad tracks. It was dark, his eyes were heavy and his body ached, but Belissari couldn't sleep. Not in the back of the uncomfortable buckboard. Not when he was unsure where these men were taking him.

To the south lay nothing but the Chihuahuan Desert, maybe a hundred miles to the Big Bend of the Rio Grande and beyond that, Mexico. It was some of the hardest country Belissari had known, a region of unsettled, unholy land, breathtaking yet brutally inhospitable. The riders picked their way over cacti, through canyons, and up and down hills as the wind whipped and coyotes cried.

Belissari's stomach suddenly tightened. *This would be the perfect spot to dispose of a dead body.*

By ten after seven, Hannah Scott knew something was wrong. Pete Belissari would not be late. Her stomach churned uneasily as she recalled Pecos and several other Malady riders bolting out of town. She tried to tell herself that she was being outrageous, that the horseman would round the corner at any minute.

Her hands were clammy, her heart heavy, but she forced herself to sit on the bench for ten more minutes just in case. *Seven o'clock. Lempert Hotel. I'll meet you there,* Pete had said. She pictured his face, smiling, but the image was quickly obscured by that of the buckboard racing southward.

She rose quickly and pushed her way down the crowded boardwalk, eyes suddenly blazing, sure that the horseman had been kidnapped. *If they hurt him* . . . she began, but lost the thought when she almost trampled two soldiers walking out of Lightner's Saloon. She shoved her way past the startled men and only stopped when she realized who they were.

"Doctor Leslie!" she shouted, turning on her heels. The old man removed his hat with one hand and cigar with the other and graciously bowed. The other officer, Belissari's friend Captain Kaye, tipped his kepi politely and smiled.

"Did y'all see Pete today?"

"Why, yes, ma'am," the doctor said. "Aren't you supposed to be dining with him tonight?"

"He didn't show up. Something's happened!"

Kaye's smile vanished, but the doctor remained unconvinced. "I wouldn't worry too much, Miss Scott," Leslie said. "That boy will turn up soon."

"Something's wrong!" Hannah was furious. These two men were supposed to be his friends. "Pete was supposed to meet me at seven, and about a half-hour ago I saw some of Rafe Malady's men hightailing it out of town with a buckboard."

"Ma'am," Kaye began, but Hannah cut him off.

"I tell you something's wrong! I need your help."

"Child," Leslie began, his patronizing tone infuriating her. "Pete hasn't slept in I don't know how long, more than two days. He probably just fell asleep somewhere."

She was so mad she almost cried, but she wouldn't do it in front of these men. "Something's wrong!" she repeated and turned abruptly from them, hurrying down the boardwalk. "I thought you two were his friends."

Leslie shook his head and returned his hat and cigar. "That girl worries more than my wife. Poor Petros is going to be in for it if he has overslept." He laughed and glanced at Kaye.

The captain's eyes were trained on the bouncing red bow above Hannah's waist as she hurried away. "Pete wouldn't oversleep," he said, softly stroking his whiskers.

"You think that girl's right?"

"I don't know," Kaye replied. "Check with Sergeant Major Cadwallader when you get back to the fort, Jack. Pete was supposed to sleep in our corrals tonight. If he's not there, tell Cadwallader to find me, maybe give a couple of his best troopers some passes. I'm going to poke around town."

The buckboard had stopped in the darkness. A white glow shone behind a mountain and Belissari watched as he frantically worked his hands and wrists behind his back, desperately trying to free himself quickly. By now he was sure that Pecos and his men meant to kill him.

The shine increased and suddenly a giant moon appeared, casting shimmering white light as it climbed in the desert sky. Belissari could see clearly now, for the moonlight was as bright as morning. The buckboard driver was licking one of the peppermint sticks Belissari had bought for the children, Pecos was in the bushes overlooking a gully, and the rest of Malady's men were standing by their horses, passing a bottle of whiskey and laughing.

Pecos returned now and Belissari's shoulders sagged. He had gained no ground on the ropes; whoever tied him up knew what he was doing. The tall gunman nodded at the driver. Belissari tried to swallow but his throat was like the desert. He turned quickly to face the cowboy but was too late. He saw the flash of a gun barrel in the moonlight and felt it crash above his right ear.

The horseman toppled on his side, pain blinding him, tears welling. He gritted his teeth, then relaxed as his mind went numb, drifting into oblivion. For the first time since Wednesday night, Pete Belissari slept.

She had gone back to the Reverend Cox's to change into something more comfortable and sobbed on the old minister's shoulder as she relayed her fears, then returned to town, walking up and down the streets, checking every hotel, livery, and boardinghouse, asking strangers and friends alike if they had seen Belissari. Now she was peering into the saloons though she knew it was unlikely Pete would be in one. But she also thought she might find Buddy Pecos or Rafe Malady.

If she found one of them or any of Malady's men, she'd make him talk. Her father's Navy Colt had blown up in her hand, but she carried a Remington derringer in her purse. The Reverend Cox had given it to her before she left.

She was resting underneath a gas street lamp, collecting her thoughts, when she saw a sheriff's deputy heading her way. He was leading a saddled gray horse behind him. Her heart raced. *Poseidon!*

Hannah charged the deputy, startling him so that he almost swallowed a giant plug of tobacco he was chewing. "Where'd you find that horse?" she screeched. "Where are you taking him?"

The deputy gathered his wits. "He was just wanderin' over by Lempert's Addition," the man said in a slow Texas drawl. "Reckon folks think they can just let their horses wander 'bout town 'cause of the race and crowds, but nosireebob. That's a dollar fine."

"How 'bout the owner?"

"Little lady, if I knowed the owner, I'd just make him pay me and tell him to stake his horse somewhere. I done told you the horse was just wanderin'. All the livery stables are full, so the sheriff told me to find this horse and take care of him. Said the county will pay me back."

He moved past her and Hannah stared at Poseidon. There was no blood on the saddle, no sign of trouble or violence, but one rein had been broken. She patted the horse's side as he walked by, then ran toward Lempert's Addition, loping around a corner and almost running over Captain Vernon Kaye for the second time that night.

Kaye caught her in his arms. Her chest heaved and she wiped her eyes and told her about Poseidon. Kaye frowned.

"What is it?"

"Charles Buehler said some of Malady's cowhands got into a fight in the alley behind his bakery this evening. He also said Pete bought some stick candy just before the fight."

"The bakery's near the Addition," Hannah said.

Kaye nodded. "Buehler didn't see the fight, just heard it. When he stuck his head out the door, the sheriff told him it was two cowboys. Buehler recognized some of Malady's men as they rode out after the fight."

"The sheriff is in Rafe Malady's coat pocket!" Hannah was furious.

Kaye just nodded. "So it could have been Pete."

"It was Pete."

Kaye sighed heavily. "I think you're right. You said they rode south."

Hannah nodded, dabbing her eyes with her shirt-sleeve.

"Malady's brother lives in Marfa. Or they could have taken him somewhere else, could have doubled back to Malady's ranch." *They could bury him in the desert,* Kaye thought, but he didn't say it. "That's a lot of country to cover."

"You have the entire Army—"

"Hannah, I don't have the Army." It was the first time Kaye had used her first name. "This is not an Army matter. I have three soldiers and me, and if my commanding officer finds *that* out, I'm in deep trouble. We should leave one in town in case they're holding Pete here, or if we're all wrong."

"I can ride."

"That gives us four. That's not enough to cover the territory. We need more help."

Hannah tightly closed her eyes. The two were silent for a minute. Kaye shook his head and said, thinking aloud more than anything, "I'd kill to have a good tracker right now."

Hannah nodded. She heard boot heels on the boardwalk and looked up. Four men were walking toward them, their cigars glowing. As they walked forward, a streetlight revealed their faces and lit up Hannah's.

Belissari coughed and snorted, spitting out water and blinking rapidly. His eyes stung. The giant moon glared at him in roughly the same spot he remembered before being knocked out. He had been unconscious for five, maybe ten minutes, during which time they had moved him to the edge of the gully and untied him. Then someone had drenched him with water.

"You don't want to sleep through this, mister," a cowhand said, prompting laughter from everyone but Pecos and Belissari.

Pecos towered over Belissari. "Ride out," Pecos ordered his men, stilling the cackles.

"But, Buddy—"

"I said ride. I'll catch up."

When the sound of the horses was distant, Pecos knelt beside Belissari, who managed to push himself into a seated position on the desert floor. For a few minutes, only the wind and coyotes spoke.

Finally Pecos said, "I have nothin' against you, mister. I just ride for the brand." His voice was apologetic, but Belissari was in no mood.

"That don't make killing me right."

Pecos's eyes burned. "Back up, Belissari." His voice was a dry whisper, deadly sounding. "I could have killed you when you were on that barn roof. I had you dead to rights in that canyon. And I heard you long before you saw me after your set-to at Maggot's. The only reason you're alive now is because, well, I respect you more than I respect my boss. Another time, another place, we might have been pards."

Belissari said nothing.

The gunman smiled and pointed to his ugly face. "In the war," he said, "I enlisted in the artillery. Learned all about windage and elevation. But my captain was a drunk, and one day he decided to light his pipe while sitting on a keg of powder. That's how I got this beauty. Then I got to be a sharpshooter, taught myself how to kill with my Sharps. My captain this time was a gutless coward, and I hated him. But he was my commanding officer, and I just follow orders.

"So now Rafe Malady's my captain. He told me to kill you and dump you in the desert. I hate Malady's guts, but, like I said, I ride for his brand. A man has to be loyal to his outfit." Slowly Pecos rose.

"You're wrong, Buddy," Belissari said. "A man only has to be loyal to himself."

"Maybe," Pecos said. His right boot flew forward and caught Belissari square in the chest, sending him backward, toppling over and sliding down the gully. He bounced over a cactus and tumbled over, tasting gravel, rolling, picking up speed until his side crashed into a yucca plant and knocked the wind out of him. When his lungs finally worked again, Belissari struggled to rise.

He looked up and saw Buddy Pecos, silhouetted in front of the white moon, staring down at him. The tall gunman raised his Sharps rifle. Belissari had no place to run. He braced himself, apologizing to himself for letting Hannah Scott down.

The rifle boomed.

Chapter Sixteen

Puha's familiar face remained expressionless as Hannah relayed her fears about Belissari to the three Comanches and Indian agent who had stopped at her ranch Friday. She focused on the agent, Perry Anderson, but kept the Comanche leader in the corner of her eye. Something told her Puha was the real boss of this group, but she couldn't even tell if he understood what she said.

Cigar smoke drifted above Puha's black eyes as he stood beneath a gas streetlight. He was dressed in a fancy suit, while the other Indians donned buckskins. Winter Wind, the restless horseman, shuffled his feet on the boardwalk and finally flicked away his cigar. Toothless Black Bat finished his cigar and looked bored.

Her story told, Hannah nervously wrung her hands.

Anderson removed his cigar. "Ma'am, this really is a job for the sheriff."

"I've told you that the sheriff belongs to Rafe Malady. He won't lift a finger to help Pete."

"I'd like to help, Miss Scott, but you have this soldier at your command. These Comanches are my charges, and I really can't risk their necks. Why, the bureau, the president even, would tan my hide if—"

"We go."

The voice was soft but firm, carrying above the din of saloon music and laughter. All eyes suddenly turned to Puha. Those were the first words Hannah had ever heard him speak.

Puha took a long drag on his cigar and handed it to Black Bat, who quickly began puffing away. Winter Wind smiled.

"Puha," the agent began. "You can't go. The big race is tomorrow and—"

"We go." The tone was the same, but this time Anderson did not argue.

"Oh, thank you!" Hannah shouted. She leaned forward and kissed the chief on his cheek. Winter Wind yipped excitedly, Black Bat grunted something in Comanche and laughed, and Hannah finally saw Puha's face change.

"Son of a gun," Kaye whispered. "He's blushing!"

Buddy Pecos was gone. He had fired the Sharps, mounted his horse and ridden away. Yet Belissari was still standing, too stunned when the bullet missed that he hadn't even played possum. Pecos had let him live or at least given him a chance.

Belissari was on foot in the middle of the desert, stuck in a gully with no water. With luck, he could make it back to Fort Davis in a couple of days but he would have to take it easy. With bad luck, he would die slowly, painfully. Maybe Pecos hadn't done him any favor. A bullet would have been quicker.

He pushed that thought aside and headed to the edge of the gully wall, looking for a place to climb up. The moon bathed the desert with white light now and he'd take advantage of it and the cool night air. Out of the gully, he'd try to find a water hole he knew of, rest there the next day, and move on at night. If the water hole was dry . . . well, he wouldn't think about that now.

Looking up instead of where he was walking, he tripped over something on the ground. He gritted his teeth, thinking the coiled object on his right foot was a rattlesnake, but quickly realized his mistake. "Rattlesnake!" he mumbled and picked up the hemp reata. Pecos must have left it for him. He looked up and saw a boulder at the top of the gully.

Belissari unloosened the rope and hurled it upward. On his second try, the reata fastened around the boulder. He pulled hard twice, making sure the rope was secure, then climbed up. The rope burned his hands but Belissari ignored the pain and made it to the top. Beside the boulder he found an old wooden canteen, with "B.P. CSA" burned on one side.

"Buddy Pecos, you old Rebel, you do have a decent side," Belissari said to himself after taking a conservative sip of water. He wound up the reata and put it over his shoulder, then walked northward through the desert.

* * *

Four soldiers, three Indians, an Indian agent, and a woman. It was an odd search party, Hannah thought as they met in front of the Reverend Cox's house.

"We're going to split up," Captain Kaye said. "Mister Anderson, I'm leaving you in town in case they're holding Pete here." The agent nodded nervously.

"Corporal Cummings, ride to Malady's ranch and reconnoiter there. Trooper Washington, you'll need to stay in town as a galloper in case Mister Anderson discovers Pete here.

"That leaves us. They could have taken him to Marfa, where Malady's brother lives, or into the desert. Sergeant Major Cadwallader, Puha, and Black Bat will take the road to Marfa. Winter Wind, Miss Scott, and I will ride into the desert. Whoever cuts his trail will send a galloper after the other party. Agreed?"

Heads bobbed silently. "We have an Apache moon," Cadwallader said. "That should help."

"Comanche moon," Winter Wind corrected, smiling.

"Sorry. *Comanche* moon."

Kaye slowly exhaled. "There's one other thing. Washington, Cummings, if you haven't heard from us by dawn, get back to Fort Davis before reveille. Captain Leslie has us all down for sick call, but if someone finds out we're off the post, we're all in trouble. There's no need in you sacrificing your military careers."

Both soldiers nodded. "What about you, sir?" Washington asked.

"Sergeant Major Cadwallader and I stand a better chance of surviving a court-martial."

"But what if you aren't back in time for the race tomorrow?" Anderson said. "Puha, you've already paid the entrance fee."

"Then you ride him!" Puha said.

Without the moonlight Belissari would have never found the water hole a half-Lipan, half-Irish mustanger had shown him years before. He stumbled for hours. His legs ached and the wind-blown dust stung his sleep-deprived eyes. Finally, he saw the cutaway in a mountainside. Breathing easier now, he followed the animal trail. The wind moaned and the moon disappeared behind clouds. In the blackness, Belissari groped through the path, feeling his way along the cool rocks, hoping he wouldn't find a real rattlesnake.

He stepped into a clearing and smelled the water and juniper. And then he heard the water splash and a snort. *Mescalero!* he thought as his throat went dry and his lungs froze. The moon reappeared, and Belissari stared in silent amazement.

A lone mustang stallion whinnied and splashed its forefeet in the water, shook its head and drank some more. Belissari uncoiled his rope and moved forward. "Easy, boy," he said softly as the horse's head jerked up, ears pointed. Belissari walked slowly, his voice smooth. The stallion snorted again, shook its head, and danced to the left and right.

Suddenly the animal bolted and Belissari let his reata fly. It moved effortlessly over the mustang's neck and the horseman braced himself but was jerked to his knees. He was dragged a few yards, but recovered and wrapped the rope around the juniper.

The lariat held. The mustang snorted and screamed, rearing and pounding the desert floor with savage— and deformed—forefeet. He was splayfooted, Belissari noticed, an affliction that caused his forefeet to be toed out. It was a condition that could be fixed with proper shodding but until that time the horse would always have a bizarre duck waddle for a gait.

He let the horse's anger subside, then approached it, softly singing an old gospel song. He pulled the money voucher from inside his shirt and stuffed it in his pants, then peeled out of his shirt. The horse stepped back some, eyes flaming, and Belissari tossed his shirt over its head. Blinded, the horse immediately calmed down, but Belissari continued to sing and softly patted the animal's neck.

Now what? he thought. He had a splayfooted nag, but neither bridle nor saddle. The horse was branded, but Belissari didn't recognize the mark. He guessed that Apaches had stolen the horse from some hacienda in Mexico years ago and it in turn had escaped the Indians. The burrs in its ragged mane and tail told him the mustang had not been ridden in years.

There was nothing he could do until daylight. The horse wasn't going anywhere, and Belissari needed sleep. He was walking toward the water hole when the arrow flew past his left ear. Belissari dived to his right and heard a gun bark. He rolled behind a boulder and looked up. It was the same Mescalero raiding party he had run into days before. They had entered the water hole through some back way known only to them, and they weren't friendly.

From the corner of his eye he saw the Indian, and he ducked to his left just in time. A knife flashed downward but Belissari blocked the blow and grabbed the boy's right wrist with his left hand. His own right flew forward and cracked against the youth's jaw. The kid grunted and Belissari followed with another punch, then drove the boy back against the boulder with his weight. His right hand grabbed hair and Belissari pulled the boy's head forward, then slammed it against the rock.

The youth slid down the rock unconscious and Belissari grabbed the knife and bolted toward the mustang, his only hope. Another gunshot exploded and the horse screamed in fear. An arrow nicked the web of flesh between the thumb and first finger on Belissari's left hand, and a bullet kicked dirt into his eyes.

The Apaches yipped and charged as he reached the horse. Belissari slashed the reata holding the horse and tossed the knife away. He twisted the mustang's ear with his left hand, grabbed a fistful of mane with his right and swung on board. The mustang wheeled, but Belissari didn't fall, and then the animal was running down the trail with the Apaches right behind.

Belissari knew he had no chance. He was unarmed and on the bare back of a wild horse. And his only chance of escape had deformed feet.

Winter Wind found the trail. A wagon and several horsemen riding south fast. Captain Kaye galloped into the night to find Puha, Cadwallader, and Black Bat, while Hannah and the happy-go-lucky Comanche rode on in silence, following the trail in the moonlight.

They were well past the railroad tracks when the others caught up. A short time later, they heard the drunken banter of cowboys and squeaking wheel of buckboard with an axle in need of grease. Cadwallader rode ahead and returned with a report twenty minutes later.

"Some of Malady's riders with a buckboard. Heading north. That tall fellow, Pecos, was with them."

"The buckboard?" Hannah's lips trembled.

Cadwallader swallowed. "It was empty, Miss Scott. I had a good view with my binoculars. They were drinking, celebrating. And their horses looked tuckered out. They'd been riding hard."

"We know for certain we're on the right trail," Kaye said. "These Comanches won't have any trouble following it."

"To what?" Hannah blurted angrily. "Pete's body?" Cadwallader looked down, shuffling his feet awkwardly. Even Kaye was unable to move. Both men believed that the empty buckboard meant Pete Belissari was dead.

"He lives," Puha said firmly, softly.

Hannah's face softened. "What?" she asked, perplexed.

"He lives," Puha repeated. "We find him. We go now."

They swung into their saddles and moved south into the night. Winter Wind and Black Bat rode ahead, studying the trail. The wind picked up, and the moon disappeared.

In a matter of minutes, the wind was screaming, driving sand furiously. Heads bent low, the searchers struggled forward. The riders stopped and Cadwallader dismounted. He pulled his bandanna over his nose and mouth and struggled forward, wrapping his reata around each saddle horn and handing the end to Winter Wind. It was the only way they could keep from being separated.

Cadwallader stumbled back to his horse and climbed into the saddle. The wind screamed. Hannah leaned forward. The cold wind numbed her fingers, while at the same time the blasting sand burned her ears. She tried to block out everything and squeezed her eyes shut.

"Hannah?"

She opened her eyes, suddenly aware that the wind was no longer whipping her. Captain Kaye helped her dismount as she collected her bearings. They were in a cave, sheltered from the sandstorm.

"What now?" she asked weakly.

"We let the storm pass," he said as he led her to the fire. She crouched over the small flames and wearily dropped beside Puha and the others. The wind moaned outside.

"And then?" she asked.

"I don't know," Kaye replied. "But this storm will wipe out any tracks. I think we'll have to ride back to town, get a real search party, and try again."

Hannah nodded. She was too tired to argue, and she was done with crying. She was resigned to the fact that it was all over. She had lost the ranch, the orphanage. Rafe Malady had won. And Pete Belissari was dead.

Chapter Seventeen

Of the many legends his parents told Belissari when he was a boy, the myth of Pegasus was his favorite. He was captivated by the winged horse who sprang from the Medusa, was tamed with a golden bridle, flew to heaven, and became the constellation in the sky.

Belissari had no golden bridle, only a fistful of rank horsehair. And the splayfooted mustang he rode sprouted no wings. It ran like a duck. But—and this stunned Belissari—the stallion galloped as if he were part of the wind.

The mustang needed little guidance, which was good because Belissari had little to guide it with. The stallion would distance itself from the chasing Apaches with a sudden burst of unbelievable speed, then slow down to save its strength. When the Mescalero youths closed in again, the horse would resume its lope and leave the Indians gaping. This was one smart horse, Belissari thought. Soon the Apache horses would be too winded for pursuit.

On top of the next hill, the mustang slowed and stopped. Belissari looked behind him. In the distance, the Mescalero party had given up. One gestured angrily at the horseman and his winged duck, and Belissari smiled. Maybe the Apaches would now head back to New Mexico and the reservation there. His smile vanished as he saw dust rising beyond the Indians, too much to be from horses. Clouds were gathering, and the moon disappeared. Belissari felt the breeze picking up. A windstorm, he realized. He would have to find shelter quickly.

The mustang suddenly bucked. Belissari found himself flying over the horse, but his right hand caught the dangling loop of the knife-cut reata still hanging over the mustang's neck. The horse bolted, but Belissari gripped the reata firmly and pulled himself to his feet.

Belissari yelled savagely. The horse reared once but the mustanger jerked on the short rope and the animal stopped, snorting, panting heavily. "So," Belissari said between gasps, "that run tired you out too, eh, Duck Pegasus." He smiled again. The horse had caught him off-guard and thrown him. He could appreciate the mustang's smarts.

He patted the horse gently on the side of the neck, then led it toward some rocks about a hundred yards down the hill. They would wait out the sandstorm there. Once in the shelter, Belissari again removed his shirt and blinded the horse, slipped off the cut reata, and refastened it as a makeshift hackamore. He still had no saddle, but he figured he could make it back to Fort Davis in the morning. He suppressed a yawn and sank to his feet, holding the hackamore in his left hand as the wind howled and air turned cold. His thoughts turned to Hannah, and then suddenly something else entered his mind.

Tomorrow's horse race in Fort Davis. The winner would earn two hundred and fifty dollars, but that wouldn't cover Hannah's debt. He withdrew the government voucher from his pants.

"But I bet," he said to himself, "there will be a lot of wagering on that race."

The storm passed, leaving the desert fresh and clear underneath a blanket of stars. Hannah silently mounted her horse and followed the soldiers and Comanches back toward Fort Davis. The eastern horizon was already gray by the time they crossed the railroad tracks, and rays of soft gold and orange climbed the sky as they wearily entered town, greeted by a crowing rooster, barking dog, and two careworn, all-night revelers.

The riders drifted to the Reverend Cox's house, where Hannah slid from the saddle. As Cadwallader led her mare to the corral, Hannah thanked the Comanches and turned to Captain Kaye.

"Get some sleep, Hannah," he said. "We'll form a search party and head back out this afternoon. We'll find him."

She nodded. The door to the reverend's house squeaked open, and she caught the aroma of fresh coffee and bacon. She realized how hungry she was and politely asked Kaye and the Comanches if they would join her. She was certain the Reverend Cox would not mind. Kaye's mouth went agape and his eyes widened.

Hannah turned on her heels. On the front porch beside the elderly minister, holding a tin cup of coffee, looking half-dead, bruised, bloodied, and caked with dust—but still looking like a dream come true to Hannah Scott—stood Pete Belissari.

"What kept y'all?" the horseman said with a smile.

He was immediately mobbed. He dropped his cup of coffee when Hannah leaped in his arms and knocked him onto the porch. Then Kaye was at his side, helping the two to their feet. But by then the noise had awakened the children, and they were on top of Belissari, sending him down again as they screamed excitedly. Silent Bruce, however, stood at Hannah's side, smiling weakly but afraid to join the fracas.

"Easy, easy, easy," Belissari said, and the reverend and Kaye finally pried the orphans off him. Laughing, Kaye helped his friend up again, slapping him on his back, telling him he had a lot of explaining to do.

"We thought you were dead, pardner," Kaye said.

"I told you he lives."

Belissari turned and looked at Puha. The Comanche chief nodded politely and said, "We go now."

"Won't you stay for coffee?" Hannah said. "It's the least we can do."

Winter Wind bounced on his horse, and Black Bat gave a toothless grin. She could tell they wanted the coffee, and she hoped the Reverend Cox had plenty of sugar. But Puha shook his head. "No. We prepare for race. Good-bye."

After the Indians had gone, the crowd on the porch went inside for breakfast. Kaye told of their search, and Belissari shared his adventures with them, stopping to greet Cadwallader when the soldier entered the house.

"I caught the horse at the water hole, outran those Mescaleros, dodged the storm in some rocks, then made it here," Belissari finished. "Mister Cox told me about y'all going after me. I was going out looking for you after breakfast."

Kaye shook his head. "You are the luckiest man in Texas, Pete."

Belissari nodded. "I think I might be even luckier. That's some horse I caught."

Cadwallader exploded in laughter. "That nag I found in the corral! That's your dream animal?"

"She outran those Apaches, Sergeant Major. I think—"

"Mister Belissari, that animal is splayfooted. You must have been exposed to the elements too long."

Kaye and Cadwallader chuckled good-naturedly, then finished their coffee. The Reverend Cox excused himself, saying he had a sermon to prepare, and Hannah sent the children to get ready for church.

"We'd better get back to the fort, Sergeant Major," Kaye said. "Are you going to press charges against Pecos and those cowboys?"

Belissari shrugged. "You going to watch the race?"

"Mister Belissari," Cadwallader boasted, "I'm going to win the race."

The soldiers laughed again and headed out the door. "Get some sleep, Pete," Kaye said.

They were alone. Hannah took Belissari's right hand in hers and gave it a gentle squeeze. "You really should sleep," she whispered.

"I slept some in those rocks during the storm." It wasn't a lie, but he had only managed a few winks, just enough to refresh himself for the ride to town.

"Want to go to church with us?"

He shook his head, his mind racing, his thoughts far from the minister's house. "I'm going to scout out that racecourse," he said. "Six miles through open country . . . I think Duck Pegasus has a shot at winning that thing."

"Pete, I'm no great judge of horses, but I do know what a splayfoot is. Are you—"

"Hannah, I'm not crazy. The purse for winning today's race is two hundred and fifty dollars. Plus if I bet my voucher on me winning the race . . . Think about it. A splayfooted mustang that's been running wild for years? Going against some of the best horses and riders in the West? Can you imagine what kind of odds I'll get. Six-to-one? Ten-to-one? We'll be able to cover what you owe Malady and then some."

"And if you lose?"

He was on his feet now, heading out the door. "Hannah," he stated, "we have nothing to lose."

Belissari wasn't alone when he scouted the course. A Kentucky gambler and horseman named Korby Hennesy rode with him. Hennesy had been in Fort

Davis for a week, had rented out an entire livery for his thoroughbred and had ridden over the course every day since arriving. He was giving the track one final going over when Belissari joined him.

"Not afraid of giving out any secrets?" Belissari asked.

Hennesy smiled. "The race, my friend, is nothing but a roll of the dice." His accent was as smooth as blended whiskey. He gestured at Poseidon. "I trust you aren't entering that fine gray you're riding. He's a great animal, but I'd dare say he isn't a racer."

Belissari shook his head. He decided against telling Hennesy about Duck Pegasus. The gambler was on a rented horse. No doubt, the Kentuckian's thoroughbred was in the livery being attended by the best trainers Fort Davis had to offer.

The course, lined with red, white, and blue streamers, started at the courthouse in town, went down the street, and past the fort where it veered west down a hill before leaving the road and crossing Limpia Creek between a stand of cottonwoods. The water was high, but not in flood stage, nor was the current swift as it was farther north. There the course led into a pasture, going underneath more cottonwoods. A hundred yards later, the horses would be forced to jump two dead trees in rapid succession, each hurdle about four feet high.

After two furlongs through open country, the path circled a palisade of lava rocks, climbed another hill, turned sharply downward, forded Limpia Creek again, and returned to the main road. From there it was a two-mile dash down the winding road, past the fort and to the finish line at the courthouse.

Six miles. Part sprint, part marathon, all stampede, with plenty of hurdles. Even the best jockey on the surest-footed horse alive would have trouble on this course. Still, Belissari thought his sorry-looking mustang would have as good a chance as any. It was used to running in rugged country.

The two men rode back to town, where Hennesy offered to buy Belissari some sour mash at the Headquarters Saloon. Nine o'clock was a little early for Belissari to be drinking, so he politely declined.

"You wouldn't know if anybody's taking bets on this race?" Belissari asked.

Hennesy grinned. "There's a Malady running the show out of Stockmen's Palace. John Malady."

That would be Rafe Malady's brother, Belissari thought. If the brothers were anything alike, Belissari wasn't sure about the honesty of the betting, but Hennesy seemed to read his mind. "Oh, I'd dare say the bets and payoffs won't be a misdeal," Hennesy said. "I ran into the state attorney general yesterday, and the United States marshal out of El Paso. This race is drawing quite a crowd."

They wished each other luck, and Belissari returned to Cox's house.

He would see how Duck Pegasus liked a saddle and bridle. He decided against shoeing the horse. As he worked with the animal, he thought about his competition. Hennesy was a lithe, agile man, obviously smart and sure of himself. Sergeant Major Cadwallader was as fine a horseman as you'd find in the Army, and he had seen the Comanche Winter Wind ride that sleek *manoblanca* called Ecahcuitzet. Plus, Rafe Malady was rumored to own a fast runner and was no slouch on horseback himself. And, like Hennesy said, this race was drawing quite a crowd.

Twice the mustang threw him when Belissari tried to get the stallion used to the saddle, but the horseman had expected that. Duck Pegasus had been ridden years ago; of this, Belissari was sure. But years in the wild turned the stallion ornery and independent, and it would take awhile for him to become reacquainted with domestication. Unfortunately for Belissari, he didn't have much time.

The church bells chimed twelve times. He had ninety minutes before the race.

Chapter Eighteen

The boardwalks of Fort Davis were swarming. Hannah had never seen so many diverse people in one place. Cowboys, Chinese railroad workers, gamblers, children, and ministers. Mexican farmers in white cotton and vaqueros in botas, sashes, and open-sided, embroidered pants. Black and white soldiers from the fort, some in campaign fatigues, others in dress uniforms and flashy helmets. Townsmen still donning their Sunday best, others in canvas pants and homespun shirts. Trappers in buckskins. Drummers in sack suits. Women in church dresses, formal gowns and, like Hannah, plain calico.

She was awestruck as she walked with Belissari toward the courthouse. The horseman pulled the saddled, smelly, and comically clopping stallion behind him, and when he handed the reins to a race official

149

and said he was entering the event, the nearby spectators hooted and howled. Hannah couldn't blame them. Belissari smiled.

John Malady had moved his betting table out of the Stockmen's Palace and into the street to drum up more business. Whereas Rafe Malady was a short, solid, rough-cut man, his brother was tall, slim, and impeccably dressed in a gray striped suit and a perfectly tied black silk cravat. He was tailored to be a gentleman lawyer, hosteler, and banker, but people said he ruled Marfa with an iron will and was as slippery as axle grease—only harder to clean up. In that regard, he was just like his brother.

Belissari pulled out his Army voucher and waited in line, ignoring the catcalls from the crowd. Rafe Malady stood behind his brother when Belissari placed the paper on the desk.

"You take this?" Belissari asked.

"We deal in cash," Rafe Malady replied.

A man cleared his throat behind Hannah and the horseman. "That voucher, Mister Malady, is as good as cash. As the state attorney general and friend of the United States Army, I can guarantee that."

He was a squat, chubby man with a ruddy complexion and plaid suit, overshadowed by the bearded Army colonel and mustached man in black broadcloth towering behind him. The attorney general's green eyes beamed. The mustached man reached into his coat pocket and withdrew a cigar, subtly revealing a U.S. marshal's badge pinned to his vest lapel.

"Very well," John Malady said. "How much of this do you wish to bet?"

"All of it," he said, "on my late entry, Duck Pegasus, to win."

The gasp was audible. The marshal dropped his cigar, and the attorney general cried, "My world, son, don't you think that's a bit rash?"

"Odds?" Belissari calmly asked.

John Malady stared at the splayfoot, pinched the bridge of his nose, and shook his head. "Three-to-one," he said. Rafe Malady stormed away.

"Three-to-one?" Belissari was amazed. "I figured to get better than that."

"I haven't seen that horse run," Malady said, "and most of these bets have been even-money. It's hard to give odds on a race like this. So take it or leave it."

Belissari nodded and accepted a receipt. The attorney general, Army officer, and marshal shook their heads and disappeared into the crowd. Belissari handed Hannah the receipt and walked back to Duck Pegasus, where he was given a pencil and piece of paper. He scrawled on the paper and turned in the form at a scorer's table on the courthouse lawn.

The man looked it over carefully, nodded, and said, "That'll be thirty dollars."

Hannah groaned. She had forgotten about the entry fee. But Belissari calmly said, "It'll be here in a few minutes." He turned to Hannah and explained that the Reverend Cox was bringing the money. Hannah sighed and smiled, but the smile died when Rafe Malady's voice echoed: "Entry deadline is in one minute. If you don't pay now, you don't run the race."

Belissari turned savagely toward Malady, who stood smugly behind the scorer's table. "Nice job, horseman,'' Malady said. ''You just bet on a horse that's about to be disqualified before the race's even run!''

A coin landed on the table. The gold glinted as the twenty-dollar piece rattled as it spun and toppled on top of Belissari's entry form. Another piece followed, bounced high, and spun crazily before the clerk at the table slapped it flat.

A thick drawl pasted the air like fog: ''Reckon that'll cover it?''

Rafe Malady exploded. ''Pecos! Pick up that money!''

The lanky gunman eased his way to the table and pointed to the timid race clerk. ''You owe me ten bucks change,'' he told the sweating man.

Malady's voice thundered like cannon fire: ''Now, Pecos!''

Ignoring his boss, Pecos tapped his fingers on the table. ''Mister,'' he said, ''my change?''

The official's eyes darted from Pecos to Malady to Hannah and Belissari, then back to Pecos and Malady, and finally settled on Pecos. He reached into a box, withdrew two five-dollar bills, and handed them to Pecos.

''You're fired, Pecos! Be out of this county by tonight. Or you're finished!'' Malady's ears were scarlet, his face even brighter as he turned sharply and shoved his way through the spectators.

Pecos glanced at Belissari. ''You owe me thirty dollars,'' he said.

Hannah couldn't tell if the gunman were joking or not.

*   *   *

His stomach felt as if it held a slithering diamond-back turning over and over. Hannah smiled reassuringly, wished him luck, and walked away to find a spot to watch. He tried to swallow, but he had cottonmouth, so he filled his lungs, swung into the saddle, and found his place at the starting line. Duck Pegasus was suddenly hard to control. Belissari swore at his bad luck for he was stationed beside a Mexican vaquero named Gomez who was mounted on a fine white dun mare, and Duck Pegasus was busy showing off, pawing the ground, shaking his head, snorting, dancing, and occasionally trying to take a bite out of the neck of the fifteen-hand buckskin gelding to his left. The cowboy on the buckskin swore at Belissari. The nearby spectators only laughed.

Ten horses were entered in the derby, and between Duck Pegasus's bucks, Belissari managed to make a quick assessment of his competition. He quickly ruled out the buckskin. Its rider was white as alkali dust and the gelding looked bored. The dun mare looked to be a spoiler, and Belissari knew Gomez by reputation. A vaquero from Hacienda de la Raza near Juarez, he was considered one of the top caballeros in northern Mexico.

On Gomez's right, Cadwallader sat poised on the big dun Belissari had captured in the Van Horn Mountains. The sergeant major knew the area well, and horses. Even though Belissari didn't really think the dun could outrun Duck Pegasus, he couldn't help but worry about Cadwallader's horsemanship. Next to Cadwallader was a claybank quarter horse. The horse and rider came from a ranch in Nebraska. Belissari knew nothing of the cowboy jockey, the horse's owner, or the claybank, but he didn't think a quarter horse could win a six-mile race.

There was a roan, which looked to have mostly Arabian in its blood, and beside it was a chestnut quarter horse. Belissari recognized the quarter horse's brand as that of one of the big ranches near Corpus Christi, and he had done some horse trading with the roan's owner, a Duke Hoffman from Jefferson in East Texas. Both animals were magnificent—but not in a marathon race.

The gambler Hennesy sat on a blood bay thoroughbred, outfitted with a jockey's saddle. Hennesy's dapper attire had been traded in for lightweight trousers, shirt, and shoes. He saw Belissari and smiled.

Belissari returned the grin, but inside he wasn't smiling. The thoroughbred was awesome, and the gambler knew the course, probably better than anyone—even Cadwallader. A thoroughbred could handle the distance better than a quarter horse or mustang, and Hennesy appeared to know as much about horses as he undoubtedly did about poker and faro.

Winter Wind, clad in his Comanche buckskins, sat comfortably on a saddle blanket atop Lightning Flash's back. Belissari had seen that blood bay up close. At nineteen hands, its height alone would give it a big advantage, and the Comanches were reputed to be the best riders of any Indian tribe. Having seen Winter Wind ride, Belissari had no reason to doubt that.

And then there was Rafe Malady. The rancher had entered a towering Arabian, solid black except for a shock of white on its forehead. Malady looked determined, eyes intent on his task, quirt held firmly in his right hand. For a heavy-set man, Malady looked light in the saddle, and a giant Arabian had as good of a chance as any horse in this race.

Somebody's pocket watch chimed on the half-hour. It was one-thirty. Race time, but they were getting a late start. First came what Vernon Kaye called "the speechifying." The Reverend Cox gave a blessing, praying for the safety of the riders and horses, and thanking God for the beautiful day. John Malady jokingly gave some tips to his brother—the crowd laughed good-naturedly—and introduced the Fort Davis mayor, who was not about to let a gathering this size get away without doing some stumping.

Belissari ignored the politicking and praising, focusing on his task. His mind raced through the course, recalling every obstacle, every turn as he tried to form a strategy. The key, he determined, was to get out in front early. River crossings and hurdles could create a bottleneck, and he didn't want to be slowed down against the likes of Winter Wind's Lightning Flash, Korby Hennesy's thoroughbred, and Rafe Malady's Arabian.

Next, the Fort Davis band played "The Yellow Rose of Texas" and "The Battle Hymn of the Republic." Duck Pegasus bucked a little harder at the sound of the brass instruments, so Belissari was relieved when the mayor invited his daughter to come on the podium and sing "I'll Take You Home Again, Kathleen."

After the soft Irish ballad, the mayor brought up the United States marshal from El Paso, who quickly—and for this Belissari was thankful—introduced the attorney general. The attorney general said this was a great day for Fort Davis, a great day for Texas, and a great day for racing, then lamented how the governor couldn't be here to say these glorious words.

At this, the marshal stepped back on the podium beside the attorney general. He pulled his revolver from a shoulder holster, thumbed back the hammer, and aimed the barrel high over his head. The attorney general continued: "Gentlemen, good luck, and may the best man—and best horse—win."

He paused. The crowd cheered. *Get on with it,* Belissari thought. He swore silently and ground his teeth as the rattlesnake in his belly increased its writhing tenfold.

"At the count of three," the attorney general said. "One . . . two . . ." His last words were lost as the pistol shot thundered and echoed off the buildings and mountains.

Duck Pegasus bucked at the report, slamming his left hip into the buckskin's side. Horses bolted down the street, men and women cheered, and somewhere a baby cried. Belissari lashed out at his mustang with long reins and kicked him hard in the sides. The horse regrouped and charged forward, but the delay had been costly. Already, the mounts of Hennesy, Malady, Winter Wind, and the quarter horses from Corpus Christi and Nebraska had soared out front. Even the buckskin Duck Pegasus bumped recovered quickly and shot ahead.

Belissari was staring at a cloud of dust as his mustang waddled after the horses. And he knew that, unless Duck Pegasus indeed sprouted wings, he had already lost the race.

Chapter Nineteen

The cheering crowd was a blur of colors clouded by dust as Belissari galloped down the street. His hips rolled in the saddle despite Duck Pegasus's strange gait, and he leaned forward, whipping reins left and right. His hat blew off his head and bounced across his back, the latigo stampede string tugging at his neck and the wind blowing his hair and pulling at his bandages.

Practically blinded by dust, he galloped by the bank and wagon yard, loped past the fort, and veered down the hill where the road turned west. He expected the other horses to be long past Limpia Creek, so when he rounded the turn to cross the stream he was shocked at what he saw.

The horses and riders were bunched at the crossing. He heard the screams of men and mounts. Two horses

157

were down, a riderless chestnut was heading for parts unknown and a cowboy—possibly the Nebraskan—was floating downstream, his piercing cry bouncing off the granite rocks: "I can't swim! I can't swim! Help me!"

Two soldiers ran after the panicking cowboy as he splashed and tossed in the water. Belissari swung wide of the mayhem, forded Limpia Creek without a problem, and surged onto the bank, chasing the buckskin that had been next-to-last before the mayhem.

Belissari didn't have the time or desire to figure out what had happened at Limpia Creek. He was in second place, and he knew the quarter horse in front of him would fade before long. Later, he learned that the Nebraska claybank and Corpus Christi chestnut reached Limpia Creek first, but the claybank stumbled in the water and was rammed by Duke Hoffman's roan. That sent both horses down and dumped the Nebraskan in the creek, which caused the chestnut to buck as the other horses arrived and began to mill in midstream. Hennesy's thoroughbred reared, adding to the confusion. The Corpus Christi cowboy flew from his saddle and dirtied his shirt while his mount raced across the pasture.

Thank you, Apollo, Belissari thought as he charged after the buckskin. A fast start by Duck Pegasus would have placed them right in the middle of the fracas. Now he was closing in on the fast-fading quarter horse. The cowboy raked his giant rowels deeply across the buckskin's sides. The fool was going to ride that horse to death, even though it obviously couldn't win. Already, the buckskin was stumbling, lathered, breathing heavily.

"Give it up!" Belissari shouted as he flew past the cowboy. "He's finished!" The cowboy glared, digging his spurs deeper, but the gelding collapsed and pitched his rider to the ground. Pounding hooves soon sounded behind him, and Belissari leaned forward, gritted his teeth, and saw a horse and rider sail past him like a swooping eagle.

It was the Comanche on Lightning Flash.

More horses rumbled and suddenly Hennesy was beside him. The two men barely glanced at each other. Hennesy shook his head and nodded toward Winter Wind, already fifty yards in front. Belissari had underestimated Lightning Flash's endurance. And then Winter Wind, as he was prone to do, began showing off his Comanche riding skills.

Effortlessly he leaped off his saddle blanket, twisting in midair, and landed on the horse's back, only now the Comanche brave faced Belissari and Hennesy. Winter Wind flaunted his braided locks at the two horsemen, grinning mischievously.

Belissari smiled at the Indian's audacity. Bragging was fine, but it was about to land Winter Wind one big headache.

The cottonwood trees were coming up fast, only Winter Wind wasn't looking. He did his midair leap and turned—but too late. A low limb caught him in the chest and sent him hurling to the ground.

But the Indian was up in a hurry and sprinting after Lightning Flash as Belissari and Hennesy shot past him. Belissari swore a little to himself as he gained on Lightning Flash. The horse was well trained. Most animals, running at that speed, would have continued without a rider, but Lightning Flash slowed and stopped only a hundred yards from the cottonwoods near two fallen trees.

Duck Pegasus leaped the first dead tree without a problem but stumbled on the second hurdle, almost spilling Belissari from the saddle. That allowed Hennesy's horse to pull in front and sprint toward the lava rocks about a quarter of a mile away. Belissari sucked in a quick lungful and kicked Duck Pegasus forward.

Hooves echoed again behind him, and Belissari forced himself to look back. The two duns and Malady's Arabian were charging forward; farther back was the Comanche, remounted on a hard-running Lightning Flash. Belissari licked his chapped lips and let Duck Pegasus run at his own pace. It was a marathon race, and he wasn't even at the midpoint, so he figured to save the splayfoot's energy at least until they returned to the road.

Gomez's dun pulled astride with Belissari and stretched ahead; Cadwallader bolted by without a word. As they approached the rock palisade, Rafe Malady caught up with him. Belissari shot a quick glance at the black Arabian. Malady was holding in the great beast, saving its energy for the final sprint.

They galloped behind the high rock walls, out of view of the few spectators this far from town. Belissari suddenly felt a sharp stinging on his cheek. Reflexes sent his right hand to his face, where he felt warm blood running into his thick beard. Malady grinned with satisfaction. He held his quirt high as the Arabian pulled ahead and rounded the circle of rocks.

Belissari tried to ignore the burning sensation and concentrated on riding. Ahead of him, Gomez and

Cadwallader were gaining on Hennesy while Malady loped along easily. The two duns climbed the short hill abreast and tried to round that sharp, downward turn together. Belissari cringed as Gomez's mount bumped Cadwallader's dun and sent the sergeant major and his big horse stumbling and sliding down the hill in an avalanche of gravel and dust.

Duck Pegasus waddled up the hill a few seconds later and Belissari slowed the stallion, hollering, "Cadwallader? You all right?"

The soldier, covered with sweat and dirt, was kneeling to check the dun's right forefoot. "Yeah! Go on!" Cadwallader's voice boomed angrily. "That thoroughbred's fading!"

Belissari pushed the mustang down the hill and crossed Limpia Creek again, climbing back up to the main road. Gomez, Hennesy, and Malady were a half-furlong in front with two miles to go. Water splashed behind him and he realized that Winter Wind wasn't out of this race either. Kicking Duck Pegasus repeatedly, Belissari rifled after the lead horses.

He was really moving now, faster than he thought possible, gaining on the leaders with each step. Belissari could almost feel Lightning Flash's breath on his back, but Duck Pegasus somehow found an extra burst of speed and pulled away. The mustanger's mind raced back to that night in the desert when he outran those Mescaleros. Each time the Apaches drew close, Duck Pegasus loped harder. Maybe the horse was drawing on its instincts now, trying to escape the pursuing Winter Wind.

Ahead of him, the dun, black, and blood bay horses climbed the hill and turned down the main road.

Something darted across the street—afterward, many
said it was a cat, some a dog, others a small coyote—
and Hennesy's thoroughbred shied at the sudden
movement, stumbling onto its knees and catapulting
the Kentucky gambler into a hitching post in front of
the corrals at Fort Davis.

A second later, Gomez was unexpectedly thrown
from his mount and landed with a thump, clutching
his throat. Cursing and shouts reverberated as Belissari charged onto the scene. Hennesy was already up,
walking toward his thoroughbred despite an arm that
was obviously broken, but the horse appeared unhurt.
Belissari actually felt sorry for the gambler. Hennesy
had spent a small fortune on the race, had studied its
course like a lawyer preparing for an important case,
and had been in front and probably could have won
the race if not for some scared animal scurrying
across the road at an inopportune time.

A crowd of soldiers' wives and a burly blacksmith
gathered over poor Gomez. The Mexican was coughing and blood trickled through fingers grasping his
throat. The blacksmith hurled an angry oath at Rafe
Malady's direction. Belissari only glimpsed this as he
raced down the street, but he knew what had happened. Rafe Malady had used his quirt on Gomez,
catching the vaquero across the throat and pulling him
from the saddle. The rancher was getting brazen this
close to the finish line; he had only used the whip on
Belissari when he was behind the rocks and out of
view of anyone else.

Past the fort and onto the main street, Duck Pegasus gained on Malady's Arabian. They were abreast
as they came to the wagon yard. Cheers, shouts,

groans, and hoofbeats deafened Belissari's ears. He blocked out everything until it seemed as if he could only hear his own heart pounding against his ribs and the weary snorts of the tiring stallion that had carried him so gallantly.

Fiery pain shot through his right arm and snapped him out of his dream. Again his arm burned and he heard a moan from the nearest spectators. Duck Pegasus continued his strange waddle, easily matching the gait of Malady's Arabian. Belissari glimpsed the flash to his right and this time saw Malady's quirt rip the sleeve of his new shirt and bite into his flesh.

The rancher muttered something, glanced ahead, and sent the small whip toward the horseman's throat. This time, however, Belissari was ready. His right arm shot up to protect his throat and the whip wrapped around his arm. Belissari grabbed the lower third of the weapon firmly in his right hand and yanked it toward him. At the same time, he reined Duck Pegasus to his right.

Malady's eyes went wide with surprise and fear as the horses collided. Belissari jerked hard at the crash and saw the short rancher sail into the street behind him while both horses stumbled. The horseman was aware that he was no longer in his own saddle and instinctively wrapped the reins in his left hand. He hit the ground in an discharge of dust and heard screams from the crowded boardwalks.

Duck Pegasus pulled him a few yards before stopping, and Belissari stumbled to his feet. Malady had recovered his own senses quickly and lunged toward the Arabian, which had been knocked onto its side and struggled to rise. Out of the corner of his eye,

Belissari saw Lightning Flash charging forward, but the stallion veered sharply to avoid trampling Malady or the Arabian. The Comanche horse was heading toward the boardwalk at a high lope, and the spectators exploded out of the way like dynamited quartz.

Winter Wind reined Lightning Flash to a violent stop before the horse hit the boardwalk, but the move sent the young Comanche sliding off his saddle blanket and into a water trough. The Indian recovered quickly, leaped back on the horse, and guided it toward the finish line.

Belissari's right leg throbbed and he could barely breathe as he pulled himself into Duck Pegasus's saddle and slapped the horse's side. Malady swore behind him as he struggled into the saddle, but Belissari dared not look behind him. Not this time. Not with the finish line stretching a hundred yards in front of him.

Lightning Flash pulled astride of Duck Pegasus. Malady's Arabian thundered close behind. "Go!" Belissari shouted, kicking his stallion with what little energy he had left. "Go! Go! Go!"

The horse waddled. Lightning Flash snorted. The Arabian faltered and dropped farther behind despite Rafe Malady's roars. Time ground to a halt like the hands on a cheap pocket watch. Lightning Flash and Winter Wind were incredible. The horse had been caught in the confusion at Limpia Creek, then Winter Wind had been knocked afoot by a cottonwood branch. And yet here they were at Belissari's side only yards from the finish line. Belissari thought he saw Hannah in the crowd, her hands covering her mouth, but there was nothing she—or even he—could do.

This was up to Duck Pegasus.

They were neck and neck, twenty yards from the end. Belissari stopped breathing. He was oblivious to everything but the colorful ribbons that crossed the street at the courthouse. Duck Pegasus lunged forward with one last burst of strength, Lightning Flash matched his stride, and Belissari was vaguely aware of both horses bursting through the ribbons, followed by a detonation of cheers.

Chapter Twenty

"Watch the children!" Hannah implored the minister as she pressed her way through the throngs of screaming, hysterical men, women, and children.

"Who won?" people asked over and over.

"Couldn't tell," was the common response, which was quickly followed by arguments for Belissari and the Comanche.

Her heart was pounding. She squeezed in and out of places like a mouse, dropping to her hands and knees to crawl underneath a fat, bowlegged man—not ladylike for sure, but she was beyond caring. Hannah saw an opening and ran toward a wall of men and women surrounding the courthouse. A fusillade of cheers shattered what was left of her nerves, then she tripped and fell.

Applause surrounded her, the Fort Davis band flew

into a song and a cowboy turned around, apologized, and helped her up. As she was pulled to her feet she saw someone go sailing in the air. The body descended, disappeared behind the wall of men, more yells and clapping sounded, and there was the body again, flying high then dropping amid a thunderous ovation.

"One more time!" a voice yelled. "Hip hip hurrah!"

This time Hannah recognized the flying man. It was Pete Belissari.

A mob swarmed upon him like wolves before he slid from the saddle. His tongue and throat pleaded for water, but the crowd pulled him forward, cheering, slapping him on the back, then sent him shooting into the air like a circus performer. They caught him, shouted more praise, and heaved him up again. Somewhere a band was playing "When Johnny Comes Marching Home," but it seemed a thousand miles away. Belissari was catapulted skyward again, landing safely in the arms of men, and this time was eased to the ground.

He inhaled deeply as hands slapped his back, gripped his hand, shook him violently and addled his brain. The mayor was in front of him now, working his arm like a water pump and grinning widely.

"Who . . ." Belissari tried, gasping. "Who . . . won?"

Catcalls, shrieks, and a discharge of laughter almost drowned out the mayor's reply. "Who won? 'Who won?' he says! Why, you won, son!"

Amid riotous laughter, someone pushed him forward and he was forced to shake more hands, and finally staggered into Captain Vernon Kaye's arms. "Ease up, ease up!" Kaye shouted, and the cheers slowly died. "Let the man breathe," Kaye admonished. Belissari's legs wavered and he almost collapsed. Exhaustion swept over him like dust in the desert. Someone handed him a dipper but the cool water did little to slake his thirst.

"Where's . . . where's . . ."

Kaye cut his friend off. "Trooper Washington has Duck Pegasus. He'll walk him and let him cool off, brush him down good, and give him some water and grain."

"No," Belissari whispered. "Not that."

He pulled away from Kaye and moved through the crowd. Kaye followed closely. Someone handed Belissari a mug of beer, and he drank it in two gulps to more hurrahs. He was heading toward the podium, aimlessly wandering through the crowd, but he knew what he needed.

The beer and water aided his vocal cords, and he finally breathed normally. "H-H-Hannah!" he shouted. "Hannah! Hannah!"

A beautiful woman in bright calico burst through the crowd and leaped the final yards. He swung her around—folks gave them a wide berth—and swallowed her in his arms, pulling her tightly against him. Her head tilted forward and she looked into his eyes. Pete Belissari didn't know exactly when he had fallen in love with Hannah Scott, but he knew his case was hopeless. He just realized that he had never kissed the woman.

He closed that chapter in the middle of the streets

of Fort Davis, amid an even louder ovation from the spectators.

When they pulled apart, Belissari kissed her again, stopped, and said hoarsely, "Marry me."

Hannah stepped back, startled.

"Marry me," he repeated.

"Pete." She glanced at the crowd and back at him, and for the first time Belissari saw her blush. "I think you've got sunstroke," she said slyly.

"I've never been so sure of anything in my life," he said. "Marry me."

The red in her cheeks faded, and her eyes danced. "Aren't you going to get on your knees and *ask* me?"

Now it was the horseman's turn to blush, but he took her right hand, still bandaged from when her Colt misfired, in both of his and dropped onto both knees. Caressing her fingers, he no longer felt exhaustion. The Reverend Cox stood in the crowd, the children at his side, and other smiling faces registered, but they fell out of focus as Belissari looked up into the lovely woman's features.

"Hannah Scott," he said, "I am hopelessly yours forever. I am madly in love with you and want to be with you for the rest of my life. Will you marry me?"

Her reply was immediate. "Yes, Petros Belissari. I will marry you!" The crowd cheered, and the children pulled away from the minister and tackled the horseman, shrieking with delight. Even silent Bruce was smiling. Hannah covered her mouth and tried in vain to suppress laughter through tears of joy. Belissari wondered if he would ever have the strength to stand back up.

"You!" The voice ended the celebration instantly,

and Belissari pulled himself up as Rafe Malady stormed at him, shaking a stubby finger in his face. "You're finished, horseman! You cheated in that race, and you'll not collect a dime! I'll run you out of town on a rail, you two-bit horse thief!"

"Shut up, Malady!" Malady turned toward the voice savagely, as if he were an angry bull. The rancher wasn't used to being talked to that way, but his charge was checked when he recognized the state attorney general, surrounded by the U.S. marshal and two officers from Fort Davis.

The chubby man wagged a finger at Malady. "It's you who are finished, Malady. If this young man doesn't press charges against you for using that quirt, then I'm sure Señor Gomez might. Or I'll file charges myself. Your barbaric acts have tarnished this great day, and I'll make sure you do jail time."

The official found the sheriff in the crowd. "Reilly, the marshal and I will be visiting your office later this afternoon. Make sure you're available." The sheriff only nodded. He was on Malady's payroll, but it was beginning to look like he had drawn his last gold piece.

"John," the attorney general spoke tersely, turning toward John Malady, "I know he's your brother, but what he did was a crime. And he must pay!"

John Malady nodded, but he had concerns other than his brother. Already people were waving receipts in his face, ready to collect their bets. Belissari nudged Hannah forward, and she withdrew the slip of paper that, at three-to-one odds, was worth more than two thousand dollars.

Rafe Malady bulled his way through the crowd,

away from his brother, and the attorney general shouted, "Go ahead, Rafe, run. But you can't hide from me! Not in all of Texas!"

And then it was over. The marshal told Belissari to be at the sheriff's office in an hour, and the crowd dispersed. Many headed for the saloon, others for home. A fuming John Malady told one of his men to pay off all of the bets at the bank, turned on his heel, and hurried away. Only Belissari, Hannah, the children, and the minister remained in the streets.

Belissari leaned against the hitching post in front of the Stockmen's Palace. A Malady Brothers establishment, the doors were still locked and probably would not open today, not after the beating its owners had taken.

Hannah put her arms around the horseman and kissed his cheek.

"When do you want to get married?" she asked softly.

Belissari blinked. "Tomorrow."

She laughed. "You don't give a girl much time, do you, horseman?"

"Don't want to give you time to back out."

Squeezing his hand gently, she whispered. "Darling, I'll never back out, and I'll marry you tomorrow if Reverend Cox agrees."

"I will," the minister said. "I'm Presbyterian, but open to some things. Any Greek traditions you want to throw in?"

Belissari shrugged. "We break plates at the reception and drink ouzo," he said wearily.

"Be hard to do here," Cox replied, smiling. "This

is rye country, and most plates in this neck of the woods are tin.''

''Seven o'clock,'' Hannah said, playfully wagging a finger in Belissari's face. ''Don't stand me up this time, Petros.''

She pulled him close and kissed him gently. ''I love you, Pete. I'll marry you tomorrow and . . . get some sleep, please.'' Giggling with excitement, she added, ''Oh my gosh. I have a million things to do before tomorrow night!''

He smiled as the children pulled her away. The wind blew faintly as he watched Hannah and the children follow the minister back home. His own mind raced. He needed a bath, a shave, a haircut, a suit . . . *A ring!* Gently he rubbed the bandage on his head and wondered if it would be all right to wear a hat during the ceremony. Probably not, he decided, and it didn't really matter. All that mattered was that Hannah Scott said yes.

As the orphans rounded the corner, young Bruce turned back and stared at Belissari. The horseman waved at the boy, then noticed the child's face freeze. Bruce's mouth opened and cried out a warning: ''Look out!''

Belissari ducked and turned as a machete sliced into the hitching rail. The horseman backed onto the boardwalk. Rafe Malady tried to pull the machete loose, but the blade was firmly planted in the cedar post. Malady's face was deep crimson, and he gave up the weapon, lowered his body, and sprang forward.

The rancher's shoulder caught the horseman in his stomach and Malady wrapped his arms around Belissari, driving him backward and through the plate-glass window of the Stockmen's Palace. Both men fell over the sill and landed on the floor as a shower of glass rained on them.

Chapter Twenty-one

Belissari broke free of Malady's grip as they hit the floor. Quickly he pulled himself from underneath the heavyset man, but Malady kicked his feet from under him, dropping the horseman face first on the hardwood floor. Malady was up now, eyes vacant. He slapped his right hip instinctively but neither man was wearing a gun belt. Malady cursed and charged. Belissari raised his legs and bent his knees. When his moccasins caught Malady's midriff, the mustanger rocked on his back, kicked his legs out, and heaved the rancher overhead.

Malady crashed into a table stacked with chairs, sending furniture flying, but the man was back on his feet quickly. He flung a chair wildly at Belissari but it missed wide. Churning his feet, Malady shot out again, and this time Belissari ducked and let the rancher trip over him. Again Malady rifled through the air; this time he landed on the long bar with a grunt and fell behind among the beer kegs, whiskey bottles, and—Belissari grimaced—probably a shotgun or six-gun.

He heard Malady groping behind the bar, spilling bottles and glasses, and Belissari grabbed a chair and ran toward the bar. Malady jumped up suddenly, thumbing back the hammers of a double-barreled Parker twelve-gauge, but by then the chair was airborne.

The back of the chair caught the barrels and forced the shotgun upward as Malady pulled the trigger. Belissari's ears were ringing as soon as the shotgun roared, and the black-powder smoke burned his eyes. Plaster fell from the ceiling, and the gun's recoil sent Malady staggering back against the long mirror, spilling more glasses and bottles and dropping the weapon.

Belissari hurdled the bar and sent his right fist into Malady's gut. The rancher grunted but rolled with the punch, picked up a bottle of Scotch, and slammed it into Belissari's left ribs. The horseman grunted, brought down his fist like a battle-ax, and knocked the unbroken bottle from Malady's grip.

Malady tripped over a bottle and fell, then scurried across the floor the length of the bar chased by Belissari. As soon as Malady found his feet, Belissari whirled him around and delivered a crushing blow against the man's head. Malady snorted. Belissari fought back a yelp and shook his hand. The rancher's head was harder than granite.

Belissari lashed out with a left that missed and dodged two quick short punches from the rancher.

Malady backed up some, rethinking his plan, but Belissari gave him little time. His arms were much longer than the rancher's, so he fired out a rapid succession of lefts and rights that staggered Malady and bloodied his nose and mouth.

Malady swore angrily, found another chair, and lifted it over his head. But all that did was leave his stomach open, and the mustanger buried his right fist in the man's gut. Malady grunted, dropped the chair, and reeled backward after another punch. The rancher regrouped and punched wildly. Belissari caught the man's wrist in both arms and swung the rancher around, letting go and watching Malady fly through the shattered front window.

Outside, the rancher was up in a hurry, stumbling toward the machete and working in a frenzy to remove the weapon. But Belissari was there instantly. A roundhouse right dropped Malady into the street and Belissari was on top of him, pinning his arms with his legs, leaving Malady's face exposed. He punched the face hard. Malady's eyes closed. Enraged, Belissari hit the man again. He drew his arm back, but something grabbed his fist from behind.

Belissari turned angrily, ready to meet this new enemy, only to stare into the eye patch and scarred face of Buddy Pecos. "He ain't worth it," the gunman said in his rich drawl and released his grip. Belissari lowered his fist and struggled to his feet.

A crowd had already gathered across the street, and the marshal and attorney general were running toward them. Hannah and the children waited on the boardwalk in front of the saloon. The horseman picked up his hat, brushed back his hair, and walked slowly toward Hannah. She wrapped his arms around his waist and buried her face in his chest.

He withdrew from her after a minute and looked at little Bruce. Belissari took the boy's hand and shook it. "That machete would have hurt like blazes, Bruce," he said. "Thanks for your warning."

Angelica and Paco ruffled Bruce's hair, but the boy only smiled and said nothing. He had spoken, though, to warn Belissari, which had indeed saved his life. Bruce was far from cured and a long way from becoming a talker. Belissari knew that. But this was an excellent beginning.

Inside the jail, Rafe Malady fumed. Pete and Hannah sat behind a desk. The marshal, attorney general, sheriff, a judge, and Buddy Pecos all crowded the tiny office. The sheriff was sweating, and the other men looked annoyed at Malady's ranting.

Malady hammered his words: "No one holds me in jail! No one! I've got friends in Austin and—"

"That's enough, Malady," the attorney general said. "You were looking at assault charges before, but that machete makes it attempted murder. Marshal Smith and I will testify to that. Attempted murder, Malady. That's a term in Huntsville for sure."

"Oh, I think we can do better than that," Pecos said, punctuating his words with a stream of tobacco juice that deliberately missed the spittoon and hit the sheriff's boots. And the gunman began his statement against Rafe Malady that added charges of attempted murder for hire, kidnapping, horse theft, rustling, and arson.

When Pecos was done, Malady's face was redder

than ever. Hannah thought the man might have a stroke right there. "Reilly!" he shouted at the sheriff. "Where's my brother?"

Reilly was trying to roll a cigarette, but spilled more tobacco onto the floor than on his paper. The lawman's face was pale. "He went back to Marfa, Mister Malady."

The answer spurred Malady into another tantrum. He overturned the cot in his cell, smashed the empty bedpan against the adobe walls, and bounced a tin coffee cup off the steel bars. "Does he know I'm here?"

"Aye," Reilly said.

Malady hurled icy insults at his absent brother, kicked the walls, and finally sat down on his overturned bed.

"You've got no one, Malady," the attorney general said. "Not even your own brother."

"Yeah," Malady said, his voice still carrying. "But he'll get his. I'll teach him."

So Rafe Malady began his statement and confession, implicating his brother and others in an act of revenge and hope for a lesser prison sentence. And when he was done singing, the attorney general, judge, and U.S. marshal were preparing arrest warrants for John Malady, two railroad officials, three hired gunmen, an Austin jurist, a banker from Fort Stockton, two congressmen, a Marfa stockman, and Presidio County Sheriff Mike Reilly. There were other charges of graft, bribery, corruption, embezzlement, extortion, attempted murder—enough to keep a circuit judge busy for weeks.

It seems that the Malady brothers, along with some

railroad brass and businessmen in Marfa, Fort Davis, and Fort Stockton, had planned a stagecoach line from the railroad at Marfa to Fort Stockton—and they aimed to start it up on the cheap. There was one snag, though. They needed a swing station at Wild Rose Pass, which is where Hannah Scott's ranch came into play. That was Rafe Malady's problem.

In his confession, Malady stated that when he loaned Hannah the money to help he had been legit, but then the stage line plan unfolded and he knew he had to get that ranch. "I would have had it too," Malady concluded, "if it hadn't been for that mustanger and some splayfooted nag."

U.S. Marshal Charles Smith closed his notepad. "Where's Reilly?" he asked.

The brass sheriff's badge sat on top of a pouch of Bull Durham tobacco. The corrupt lawman must have snuck out of the office while Malady was giving his incriminating statement. The judge picked up the badge and said, "Reckon he's resigned."

"He won't get far," the marshal added.

"We'll need an acting sheriff until you can hold an election," the judge said and handed the badge to Belissari.

Smiling, Belissari put his arm around Hannah's shoulder. "No thanks," he said. "I have other plans."

Pete Belissari stepped into the sunlight, pulling his hat down on his head. Hannah kissed him on the cheek and walked away, saying she had to find a wedding dress and do countless other chores before tomorrow night. The door closed to the sheriff's office, and Buddy Pecos, polishing the six-pointed brass star on his vest, stepped beside the horseman.

"Buy you a drink?" Pecos offered.

"Sure," Belissari accepted, "but give me a minute."

The three Comanches and Indian agent were riding down the street toward them, and Belissari stepped forward and waved. Agent Perry Anderson smiled, Puha looked sullen, Winter Wind was embarrassed, and Black Bat smoked a giant cigar. Lightning Flash trotted behind, looking remarkable for a horse that had run a wild, six-mile race only hours earlier.

"Congratulations," the agent said, "on your victory and impending nuptials. A capital day, I'll say, even though we lost."

Puha grunted. Winter Wind cast his eyes downward.

"Lightning Flash should have won," Belissari said. "That's the greatest horse I've ever seen. And he'll win again."

Puha turned. "Yes," the Comanche chief stated in a deep monotone. "He great. But his rider, he stupid." He popped the side of Winter Wind's head with his palm and kicked his horse forward. Winter Wind followed, and Black Bat mumbled something and led Lightning Flash after them.

"Puha will get over it. We're off to the Mescalero reservation in New Mexico to visit some of Puha's relations," Anderson said. "And maybe put together a friendly horse race." The agent grinned. "Make up for today."

"Hope you didn't lose much money."

Anderson laughed. "I don't gamble, Mister Belissari. Puha took a little bath, but he can afford it. But Black Bat made out like a Comanchero. He bet on Duck Pegasus, only he calls him *Tosauipes*. That means 'silver coin,' and he sure won some today."

The two men shook hands, and Belissari watched the group disappear around the bend and out of town.

"About that beer . . ." Belissari smiled at Pecos's drawl and pointed his chin toward the Stockmen's Palace. They crossed the street, walked down the boardwalk, and climbed through the broken window. Inside, the two men headed to the bar.

"When's the last time you slept?" Pecos asked.

Belissari had tried not to think about that. "I caught some sleep in the desert, probably dozed a bit in the saddle, and there was that time your gunman clubbed me on the head."

"I mean sleep."

"Three nights ago, I guess."

They were leaning against the bar, staring at the mirror. Belissari removed his hat and ran his fingers through his hair. The bandage in the center made him look like a skunk, his eyes were bloodshot, there were cuts on his cheek and temple, his right sleeve was in tatters, welt marks crisscrossed his forearm, and blood, dirt, and grime stained his clothes, face, and beard.

"Didn't you get tired?" Pecos pried.

"Seems like every time I was about to hit the hay, you or Malady or someone started some trouble."

Pecos tapped his badge. "Well, that ain't likely now. So ain't you tired?"

"To tell the truth, Buddy, I'm not tired a lick. How about that beer?"

Pecos smiled and walked around the bar. Belissari looked for a chair, but the furniture was still scattered from the fight, so he pulled himself onto the bar and sat on the cool mahogany. He placed his hat beside him and rubbed his neck.

Buddy Pecos found two clean mugs and filled them with beer. He saw a box of cigars behind the bar and helped himself to a handful, stuffing them in his vest pocket. The gunman took a sip from his own mug and turned back toward Belissari.

The horseman was stretched out on the bar, curled up like a baby, crushing his battered hat with his head. Belissari wasn't snoring, but his breathing was deep and steady.

"Pardner," Pecos said. Belissari didn't stir.

"Pete." He raised his voice but there was no response.

Buddy Pecos smiled. He drained the beer he had poured for the mustanger and placed the empty glass beside Belissari's moccasins. Taking his own beer, Pecos found a chair on the floor and dragged it to the broken window. He straddled the chair, took a sip from his mug, and set the beer on the windowsill.

The streets of Fort Davis were busy now as people went about their business, hit the other saloons, or got ready to go home after an exciting day. Pecos found his bandanna and resumed polishing the sheriff's star. He glanced back at the bar, where Belissari slept soundly. The mustanger was snoring softly now.

Buddy Pecos suppressed a laugh. As acting sheriff

of Presidio County, he decided that his first duty would be to make sure no one disturbed Petros Belissari tonight. The horseman needed his rest. After all, tomorrow was going to be a busy day.